LYNTON CURLS HER HAIR

By
J. Wayne Frye

**With Assistance
From None Other
Than Mr. Fitzgerald
Who Made the Roaring 20's
Actually Roar**

Note to teachers: This book is written in Canadian English, so discrepancies in the spelling of words should be explained to students. In the vocabulary section, all words are spelled in Canadian English and the definitions are based upon the meaning within the context of this book. It is suggested that a review of the vocabulary precede the reading of each chapter.

LYNTON CURLS HER HAIR

The Author

Wayne Frye's Aaron Adams series has been popular among Canadian mystery lovers since first appearing in 2005. He provides satirical political commentary to many Canadian newspapers, and his books on politics have created a great deal of controversy. He has written marketing/advertising textbooks, been a successful U.S. university hockey coach, professor, university president and served as a marketing consultant to hockey teams and motion picture companies. He has been cited for his work with inner-city gang children in the Los Angeles area and been active in the anti-globalization movement. He became a Canadian citizen in 2003 and divides his time between Ladysmith, Vancouver Island, British Columbia and Cavite, Philippines.

Other Books by Wayne Frye

Hockey Mania and the Mystery of Nancy Running Elk
Something Evil in the Darkness at Hopkins House
How Hockey Saved a Jew From the Holocaust:
The Rudi Ball Story
The Catastrophic Calamities of a Village Idiot
Fighting for Justice in the Land of Hypocrisy
Guide to Alternative Education (13 Editions)
Cataclysmic Dreams in Black and White
Introduction to Advertising
Marketing Plan Work Book
Public Relations Workbook
Advertising Lab Manual
Promotions Workbook
Advertising Design
Fall From Apocalypse
Armageddon Now
Worth
When Jesus Came to Jersey as the Son of Thunder
When Jesus Came to Canada to Lead an Indigenous Rebellion
In the Broughton Archipelago
The Girl Who Danced with the Demons of Darkness
The Girl Who Motivated Murder Most Foul
The Girl Who Said Goodbye for the Last Time
Canadian Angels of Mercy – Nurses in Times of Peril
Points of Rebellion: Aboriginals Who Fought for Justice
Chablis: Avenging Angel for the Forgotten
In the City of Lost Hope

2

J. Wayne Frye

LYNTON CURLS HER HAIR

TABLE OF CONTENTS

J. Wayne Frye   3

LYNTON CURLS HER HAIR

TO:

Ingrid Bautista
who delivered a special poem to my sweet love,
Lynton, as a favour. She is the epitome of what the
word friend means. She is Lynton's friend, and now
I am proud to say my friend as well.

And of course, as always, to my beloved muse,
Lynton Viñas,
whose smile, infectious mannerisms and vamping
motivate, delight, titillate and mesmerize all who
gaze upon her outer beauty while delighting in the
inner beauty that radiates from the soul
of an extraordinary woman.

ISBN: 978-0-9879728-8-0

Fireside Books – Victoria, British Columbia/Port Angeles, Washington
Peninsula Publishing Consortium

J. Wayne Frye

LYNTON CURLS HER HAIR

INTRODUCTION
LET'S SOAR LIKE EAGLES

Decades ago in my youth, I sat on a private pier in Merrill's Inlet, South Carolina with a famous writer and creator of the most hard-nosed detective of all time. Mickey Spillane's seven original Mike Hammer novels once were number two in sales in the entire world, only exceeded by sales of the Bible. On that day, as he sipped on a Budweiser, which I found strange, since at the time, he was famous for doing the Miller Lite television commercials, we were talking about the pain that

J. Wayne Frye 5

goes into writing. Mickey, ever the blue-collar tough guy, with disdain for formally educated writers, said, "Pain nuts, I once made a bet with a friend that I could write an entire book in 24 hours. I did it; collected the bet and then the book sold nearly 10 million copies all over the world. The pain of being creative that these upper crust writers talk about in interviews is just writers wanting to make people think it is tough sitting behind a typewriter all day and being creative. Bull, most people become writers because they are too lazy to get a regular job. Look at me, I'm loaded with money and I work a few weeks a year if I even want to do that, so I can sit out here on the pier and shoot the breeze with people like you. There is no better job in the world than that of a writer, except maybe a university professor."

I interjected with great enthusiasm and determination, "Mickey, I want to be a writer. How do I do it? Give me a few pointers and tell me how I can find out whether I have any talent or not. Help me out here."

Mickey smiled and barked, "You want to be a writer, then get your butt off this pier, go home and take an hour or two to write a story. I'll tell you whether you have any potential or not."

I went home and wrote. That afternoon, I took my prim, proper and well-behaved 6-year-old son and my precocious 2-year-old daughter back to the pier with me. As my daughter kept getting into his cooler asking for a sip of beer, he said, "That girl is something else Wayne. Does she ever slow down?"

I replied, "Only when she is asleep, but unfortunately she doesn't do much sleeping."

I handed him the story and he said, "Keep that girl still for 20 minutes, and I'll read this and tell you whether you have any talent or not."

Trying to restrain my daughter from bouncing about on the pier was like trying to corral a wild Kangaroo, but I managed to keep her under control long enough for him to finish reading the short story about a man battling a killer ram. He smiled at me and said, "You aren't bad, but you need some refining Wayne. With luck, you might get published some day." Jokingly, he continued, "You're no Mickey Spillane, and you'll never write a book in 24 hours, but you really aren't that bad a writer."

Well, he was absolutely correct. I am certainly no Mickey Spillane, but today I am going to write a short novel in 24 hours. I think Mickey would be proud of me if he were still around.

Before beginning though, I think it imperative to give some background on what you are about to read and provide a disclaimer. First, any similarity to persons alive or dead is only coincidental, as I wanted to give a few people the thrill of seeing their names used in a novel, nothing more. Of course, like most writers, many characters are based upon people with whom I have come in contact and interacted with over the years. This is a story that germinated in a mind that was stimulated by an incredible young woman who asks for little in life, despite the fact that she has had to struggle to maintain her dignity for many years. She calls herself a simple girl, but there is nothing simple about Lynton Globa Viñas. This is an extraordinary woman who is noble of spirit. She came into my life in 2013, and changed that life dramatically. Her charm, poise, self-confidence, intelligence, wit and savoir-faire brought me not only demonstrable delight, but a new passion for life at a time when I had lost hope. And, of course, listening to her sing often brings tears to my eyes, as one can sense the deep love for her fellow man this woman has because of the passion that seems to flow from every word she sings.

I hope you enjoy the story, because it is the simple rendition of that which we all need – a great appreciation for the little things that can make a person's spirits soar. So, let's all soar like eagles as we read *LYNTON CURLS HER HAIR*.

CHAPTER 1

SOLIDIFY LOVE

There was a pale yellow hue in the midnight sky of delightfulness that night, almost as if the morning bright red sun were trying to start the day early by peering into the darkness. Wayne had just returned to Canada from the Philippines where he had spent four weeks romancing a woman far younger than he. During that time, he had grown so fond of her that he actually did not want to leave. As he sat in his office that he affectionately called the *Crow's Nest,* because it looked out over the bay below and offered a view that his friend's often called "a rich man's view in a poor man's house" his thoughts were of the days and nights that had filled his emptiness and brought pleasure to him that he assumed in despair he would never have again.

Granted, part of that pleasure was physical, as his romantic life had been dormant for some time, and the beautiful young woman certainly did arouse his libido; however, it was not the physical dalliances that he most fondly recalled, but, rather, the infectious smile that manifested itself upon the face of Lynton that would light up a dark room and touch the heart of the most callous of men. It was as if it was a beacon of hope shining in the darkness that would light the way to paradise in her arms.

Wayne's office was a bit of an anomaly, because it lacked the fine furnishings and elegant taste displayed in the rest of the house. Yet, there was a quiet elegance about it despite the somewhat shabby furnishings. The place seemed to emit a certain ambiance of soft refinement of purpose. It was a room where one felt at home and welcomed, felt that there was a sympathetic ear, an understanding heart and a devotion to justice and fairness in a world where those commodities were far too scarce.

Wayne, sitting behind his computer keyboard, looked to his left out over the balcony at the calm waters of the bay where the yellow hue in the crimson sky seemed to be dancing on the gentle waves while the moonlight cast an eerie glow on the undulating dark water. He could not write, because he was waiting for that third and last call of the day from Lynton that came in every night promptly at 11:00 P.M. She called from work; often even leaving the smart phone camera on so he could actually watch her work. It was her way of letting him share time with her, time that was so valuable to him that he could never put a monetary value on it, because it was time that was like bright gold, like shiny silver, like a sparkling diamond. This was the lifeblood of his existence, because without it, he was a condemned man, a man ready for the gallows of despair.

That night, as he sat contemplating what he could get her for Valentines Day, which was only 36 hours away because of the 16 hour time differential, he recalled Scott Fitzgerald and how he had once written of how a haircut changed a woman's life. That story bounced about in his mind, which I now relate below while also exploring the extraordinary character of Lynton Viñas. Two stories will unfold at the same time, and the two of them will simply explore how an ordinary act can give one woman new-found confidence that will inflate her ego and give another incredible happiness and solidify her knowledge of just how much one man can love a woman. One act of affection can often light a fire of love that will blaze like a roaring inferno across the heart to light the world of passion.

There was once a grand dance in the small town of Asheboro, North Carolina. There was a great ballroom which consisted of a circle of fine brocade covered sofas that lined the wall of the ballroom which was right off the game room where the men were supposed to play pool, but usually spent the evening drinking and spellbinding each other with wild tales of daring-do that were more imagination than reality.

On the other hand, the dances were oriented toward the feminine element; primarily a great congregation of somewhat plump older ladies with too much makeup to try and hide the wrinkles. And, they all had an arrogant aloofness about them. After all, these were the bluebloods of Asheboro society.

As the story is oft told, the main purposes of the dances were to see and be seen. It was more elaborate show than purposeful substance. After all, what good was it to be rich if you could not be ostentatious about it, and these people were certainly rich, if not by big city standards, certainly by Asheboro standards?

LYNTON CURLS HER HAIR

It was most desirable to keep the younger set under control, because they tended to insist on more modern music, less ostentatious surroundings and less formal attire, while the bluebloods preferred more exclusive and elite faire. If these little old biddies of conventionality had their complete way, the men would have been wearing powdered wigs and the women hoop skirts.

It was absolutely necessary to keep the affairs sedate, orderly and high toned. There could be no wild-eyed frenzied dancing with everyone gyrating their hips and shaking in a disgusting manner to music that these patrons of probity termed "of the devil." Oh, and those disgusting interludes by the young set were not be tolerated by polite society. Far too often they would slip off to dark corners, sneak a kiss or two, and even, God-forbid, maybe cop a feel here and there. And even worse, there were times when gay people would show up and actually have the audacity to dance with each other in public. There were even rumours that some of these minions of menace would actually make-out in some of the cabanas around the pool. These women were determined to keep this last bastion of probity free from the influence of the modern world that simply knew no restraints. These women were defenders of virtue.

So, as is normal, those at the top of the economic pecking order think it is their duty to define morals for those beneath them. Ironically, Mrs. Foster, Mrs. Anthony and Mrs. Comstock were all having affairs with younger men and doing the very things they were now proclaiming disgusting and of the devil. Denise Beckworth was even having an affair with Mrs. Covington, and they were the two most vociferous in attacking homosexuality as an abomination in the eyes of God. As men and women waltzed about the dance floor, the hypocrisy was accompanying them along with the music.

However, the world of adolescence is too often more sensible and more thoroughly inclusive than the adult world - where convention and stable, stagnant, constant, immutable devotion to maintaining the status-quo keeps people imprisoned to the starkness of a way of life that should be tossed into the dust bin of history so that equality and harmoniousness could become the norm rather than the exception.

Why is it that the so-called good life is kept just out of the reach of the many that deserve a shot at that illusionary good life, so the few can bask in the knowledge that they are somehow better than the average Joe? Most of the people in the ballroom were devoted to keeping things exactly as they were, so they could continue their dominance.

So, into this staid environment, a few young people seemed perfectly at home. Those from families with extraordinary incomes appeared to blend in relatively easily. This stiffness of spirit was the norm for those who wanted their place among the bluebloods who thought their status was earned just by virtue of birth. Being born to the right parents can pay huge dividends.

Now, you might logically ask what all this has to do with a woman named Lynton in the Philippines, who is one of the main protagonists of this little ditty I am sharing with you? Relax, settle back and absorb what follows and you will see how one little act can change the world for two people, one a blueblood in a small North Carolina town, and the other a hard working young woman in Cavite, Philippines.

In Cavite, while the bluebloods of Asheboro were cavorting about the dance floor, a young woman named Lynton was hard at work in the beauty salon that occupied 10 to 12 hours a day, six days a week of her time. She had been on her own since she was 16, and had to make her way in the world as best as she could. She struggled and devoted herself to her studies at the Cambridge School of Law in the metro Manila area, but when her two siblings needed help with education expenses, she dropped out of school and began her life of service to those she loved and to whom she felt an obligation.

It is not the purpose of this book to discuss whether it is the obligation of one sibling to take care of other siblings, but suffice it to say that there are differing opinions about where ones obligations begin and end. Lynton never wavered from her devotion to her siblings, and she quiet adroitly adhered to the belief that, as the oldest, it was her obligation to provide at least a minimum amount of assistance. There are those people in the world who always try to do the right thing, and this was a young woman who simply believed that her duty was to those she loved more than to herself. This selflessness was the hallmark of a woman who always reached out with the hand of compassion to those in need. Unfortunately, in a world based upon greed, there are far too many needy people. In a fair world, the government would confiscate the wealth from the haves and distribute it more evenly to the have-nots, so that no one would go without the basic necessities of life and everyone would be given a fair chance to reach heights that are unfortunately only afforded the rich and powerful in a world where a person's worth is judged by the size of their bank account rather than by the content of their character. If character were the way wealth was assessed, Lynton would have been one of the wealthiest people in the world.

Lynton, as a child faced destitution, but through the benevolence of her friend Ingrid and Ingrid's mother, was given a roof over her head. So life for her was often a struggle, but through it all she maintained her dignity and determination to not let life get her down. While she was battling to keep her head above water, in Asheboro, the privileged class continued their manifestations of living a life of grandeur and ostentatious display of superiority.

We can only frown, ask questions and make satisfactory deductions from a set of postulates, such as the one which states that every young man from a family with a large income is the object of affection from young women who see attraction as a dollar sign on the highway of happiness. On the other hand, people like Lynton saw money as secondary to all other estimations of character in a man who might make a good mate. In the drama of the shifting, almost toxic world of romantic pursuit there comes a time when a medley of faces and voices sway to the plaintive rhythm of hope, charity and possibility.

The bluebloods of Asheboro had their university degrees, their fine clothes, their sleek automobiles, their mansions and their credit cards. Of course, back in Cavite, Lynton and her contemporaries led lives of quiet desperation when it came to finances, but in many ways their lives were far happier, much superior to that of the bluebloods, because they had something wealth could not purchase. What was it they had? Perhaps a short story about a poor boy might explain: One day a father of a very wealthy father took his son on a trip to the country with the purpose of showing his son how poor some people are. They spent a couple of days and nights on the farm of what would be considered a very poor family. On their return from the trip, the father asked his son, "How was the trip?"

"It was great, Dad."

"Did you see how poor people can be?" the father asked.

"Oh Yeah" said the son.

"So what did you learn from the trip?" asked the father.

The son contemplated for a bit and sighed, "A lot dad."

The father, thinking he had accomplished his task said, "So, tell me son."

LYNTON CURLS HER HAIR

The son answered, "I saw that we have one dog and they have four. We have a pool that reaches to the middle of our garden and they have a creek that has no end. We have imported lanterns in our garden and they have the stars at night. Our patio reaches to the front yard and they have the whole horizon. We have a small piece of land to live on and they have fields that go beyond our sight. We have servants who serve us, but they serve others. We buy our food, but they grow theirs. We have walls around our property to protect us; they have friends to protect them."

With this, the boy's father was speechless. Then his son added, "Thanks dad for showing me how poor we are."

Lynton and many of her friends understand the core of this story. Too many times we forget what we have and concentrate on what we don't have. What is one person's worthless object is another's prize possession. It is all based on one's perspective. It makes one wonder what would happen if the true worth of wealth were understood. Instead of worrying about wanting more, it may be advantageous to look at just how little real character those at the top of the economic ladder actually have. Of course, Professor Wayne Frye once said that if you are going to be miserable, it is better to be miserable with money than without it, but many people are not miserable whether they have money or not. In the case of Lynton, money was not at the centre of her being. The same applied for a young member of the bluebloods named Letty, but she was just as shallow as those who sought money, since she substituted vanity for money, which can be just as bad. Lynton saw the thrill in enjoying the simple things, and how simple can a new hairstyle be? Yes, a hairstyle. This is a story about how a new hairstyle brought happiness and mirth to two people from completely different backgrounds and it is also a story of how one of these people found out that a simple gift from the heart can solidify love. The other would see the tragedy in vanity.

CHAPTER 2

EVERYWHERE THEY WENT

In Asheboro, the young bluebloods frolicked about without any cares. From Eric Appleby, the dashing young man of means, to Bob Copeland, who had a prestigious Ivy League law degree, from Diane Mossy whose hair seemed to be a mirror image of Medusa's snake filled head, to Betty Ramsay who was always the most gregarious show-off at any party, the world was a whirlwind of activities centered around the country club. There's was a world without want.

LYNTON CURLS HER HAIR

With a flourish and a bang the music suddenly stopped. The couples enthusiastically clapped their approval of the music and waited for the next tune, which much to their chagrin would obviously be another waltz when what they really wanted was some hard rock to gyrate to, but this was the staid, proper and prim country club where fastidious homage to maintaining correct decorum was expected.

Don Copeland, who was home from the University of North Carolina, being by himself, strolled out onto the candle pod-lit veranda, where couples were scattered at tables, filling the lantern-hung night with vague words and hazy laughter. He nodded here and there at the less absorbed, and as he passed each couple some half-forgotten fragment of a story played in his mind, There were Jim Johnson and Louise Ditmore, who had been having a torrid love affair for almost 5 years but could not get the courage to commit to marriage, because Jim simply could not hold down a job. They looked

J. Wayne Frye

bored, as if this was more duty than anything else. Hey, he didn't have to work, but he was forced to by a father who had cut his considerable allowance in half until he got a job, or as his father called it, a position. Unfortunately, no one was hiring vice-presidents currently, and Jim Johnson simply refused to start out at the bottom or for that matter, even the middle. He needed a burled walnut desk, a high back leather reclining executive's chair, a large window with a view of the Uwharrie Mountains and a classy secretary. Anything less was simply unacceptable.

While Jim Johnson lamented the lack of executive opportunities in a small town, Lynton was working hard everyday in a beauty salon where she toiled for wages that were about average for a Filipino, but certainly not lavish. She had been a demure child who often suffered ridicule because she was just a bit different from the norm. It is not our purpose here to explore those differences, but suffice it to say that this was a young lady who endured various prejudices much of her life, especially when she was an adolescent.

Now, Lynton, who was a discerning woman and refused to accept mediocrity in herself, had always been determined to be independent when she got older, and she certainly was. She was respected by family and peers for her determination to never give into adversity. In other words, she was the exact opposite of Jim Johnson. She called herself a "simple girl," but there was nothing simple about Lynton. In fact, she was the epitome of what grandeur truly was.

Since beauty is a question of more than the physical, and not of concrete form, no one can be acutely beautiful without an inner beauty that glows in an outward way, shining through for all to see. This was Lynton. That inner beauty manifested itself in a somewhat shy woman, but one who exuded self-confidence, because she refused to bow to conventionality in the Philippines where the conventional was defined by a staid, irrefutably rigid church that exercised inordinate control over society, even dictating government policy. She saw through the hypocrisy of a church that preached love but practiced intolerance. She was a woman who believed that you never stood as tall as when you bend down to give the downtrodden a hand up. Her compassion was legendary, as was her beauty. True beauty is not related to the physical. It is the metaphysical. True beauty is about who you are as a human being, your principles, your moral compass and Lynton's compass was true north all the time, never wavering because of her principles of respect, fairness and devotion to doing the right thing. She had true physical beauty that graced her 5:2 frame with deep dark eyes that twinkled like stars on a cloudless night. Her typical flat Asian nose added a touch of the exotic. Her smooth, soft, shiny bronze skin seemed to beg for the touch of a lover. And her smile was like a moonbeam dancing across the dark waters of a lake at midnight, shimmering with delightful countenance that beckoned for an embrace of the possible in a world of the impossible. Hers was a true beauty of mind, body and soul that radiated not from outer cosmetics, but from the simple inner pleasure that comes from making a difference for those who need your voice, your passion, your time and your hand up.

Of course, most of those playing the game of arrogant, haughty sophistication at the Asheboro Country Club would look at Lynton's dark skin and listen to her less than grammar perfect English and immediately expect her to head toward the kitchen for domestic work or to grab a broom and start sweeping up. Obviously, being Filipino, she was the servant type, meant to cater to the bluebloods.

As Lynton worked diligently in Cavite, Warren Adams was bragging arrogantly to a group of men about the girls of his town and how many he had courted. There was Casey Ormond, who regularly made the rounds of dances, house parties, and charity events just to be seen. And then there was the town celebrity, or at least she thought she was, Denise Dillon, who had a brief sojourn on Broadway where she thought she was a star, but her star had certainly fizzled out long ago. And then there was her rival for celebrity status, an athlete who had been an alternate on the Olympic team, Marci Hatzic, who was actually a terrific volleyball player, but not nearly as great as she was in her own mind.

Warren, who had grown up across the street from the most beautifully adroit young manipulator among the bluebloods, Mary Maitland, in Asheboro's swankiest community, had long been "crazy about her." Sometimes she seemed to reciprocate his feeling with a faint gratitude, but she had tried him by her infallible test and informed him gravely that she did not love him. Her test was that when she was away from him she forgot him and had affairs with other boys. Warren found this discouraging, especially as Mary had been making little trips all year, and totally neglecting him. To make matters worse, all during the month of June she had been visited by her cousin Letty from Washington, and it seemed impossible to see her alone. It was always necessary to take Letty along with them everywhere they went.

CHAPTER 3

WALKING, TALKING LOSER

Much as Warren worshipped Mary, he did have a mild interest in Letty, who was actually quiet pretty in her own way. Her dark long hair however was always dishevelled and looked like rats could rest in it as it draped down over her shoulders with flayed ends that jutted out hideously and looked like they were dynamite fuses that needed to be lit. Every Saturday night he danced a long arduous mandatory dance with her to please Mary, but he had never been anything but bored in her company.

LYNTON CURLS HER HAIR

Mary touched Warren on the shoulder and said, "Do something for me sweet Warren."

Yes thought Warren, she wants something. Why else would she be nice? He replied half-heartedly, "Yes, it is time for me to dance with Letty."

"Yes sweetheart, she has been stuck with Jim Jarman all night. She needs a gallant man to rescue her from boredom," she said as she purposefully leaned over him so he could get a whiff of her intoxicating perfume.

Warren, as usual, could not deny Mary's request. "Of course Mary, I would be delighted."

Mary, ever the artful manipulator of men in all situations and at all events, said, "Ah, you are so sweet my dear."

Warren, sighed deeply, got up and said, "Yeah, sure."

Then Mary gave him a wink and that smile she used to beguile men. "You are such an angel boy. I just adore you, sweetheart."

Yeah thought Warren, I am an angel as long as I do your bidding. He wandered about looking for Letty. She was nowhere about, but there was Jim in the centre of a group of young men who were engaging in raucous laughter. Jim was bellowing, "She's gone in to fix her abominable hair that looks like it has been in a hurricane, and then I will whirl her about the dance floor until dawn I suppose. Frankly, I am tired of trying to be nice to her."

Don Copeland, through laughter, said, "We all need to hold her down and cut that stringy, nasty pile of disgusting stuff that makes me want to puke every time I look at it. She might actually be somewhat pretty under that hideous mop."

One of the men said, "Yeah, it would be fun to clip that mop."

Jim reached down and picked up a turkey leg from the buffet table that stretched out across the side of the room. Holding it, he said, "I may use this to beat that mop down to size,"

Warren howled with laughter and said, "No need for that Jim, I am here to relieve you of your duties. I am taking over."

Jim handed the extremely large turkey leg to Warren and said, "Here, you take care of the job then."

No matter how beautiful or magnificent a young woman might be, she still craves the attention of men. It is simply a natural instinct. Letty was also like that, but she lacked the savoir-faire to get men to fawn over her. She secretly desired the attention, but was a bit too unsophisticated and lacked the proper instincts and abilities to motivate that which she secretly desired. She seemed to almost dread visiting Mary, because it just made her feel more inadequate, because Mary was so skilled at getting men to fawn over her.

Meanwhile, back in the Philippines, Lynton, was very nonchalant and somewhat shy, and even appeared uninterested in men most pf the time. Of course, there was something about her that did seem to lure men into her sphere. Despite her modicum of shyness and demure actions, she was always getting stares from men who seemed to long for her. She would just shrug her shoulders and say, "I am interested in men who see more than my outer beauty."

Her friend, Ingrid, was just the opposite in most respects, as she was more talkative and also willing to play at the typical mating game with a great deal of verve and intensity. She seemed to thrive on it at times, but secretly, like Lynton, she was always looking for that "special" man to sweep her off her feet and make her feel genuinely loved and adored. That is a basic desire of most women, to find a mate, be it male or female, who will put them on a pedestal.

These two girls spent time with their friend Channa, who was a tall sophisticated strikingly beautiful woman, but had a man in her life that seemed to fulfill all her desires for companionship. When the three were together, the sparks of intensity would fly among all the men around, as the three seemed to give off a radiance like three stars sparkling in the night in unison to light up the sky with the rays of passion and a spirited fervour that glistened with hope for all who longed to bask in the glow of their womanly charms.

Among them, Lynton was the most naturally beautiful and her smile was an extension of her kind and gentle heart, which seemed to lie dormant in the broad daylight of prosperity until it slowly and methodically crept across her pursed, pouty, thick lips as its intensity seemed like a moonbeam that blazes in the dark hour of adversity.

LYNTON CURLS HER HAIR

Meanwhile, in Asheboro, Warren danced the next full dance with Letty and was constantly swatting her wild hair off his face like it was a fly buzzing about in the summer. Finally thankful for an intermission when the band took a brief break, he led her to a table near the terrace. There was a moment's silence while she unimpressively tried to act sophisticated and worldly. Her effort seemed forced and contrived. She said, "The air is a bit stale in here. It seems to hang about you and stifle your breathing."

Warren fought back his boredom and nodded his head. She was a bit stale, but who cared. He wondered idly whether she was a poor conversationalist because she got no attention or got no attention because she was just a poor conversationalist. Desperate to break the silence, all he could think of was the misery he felt just being around her. It was almost painful to sit there and listen to her. He blurted out. "So Letty my girl, when you going back home."

LYNTON CURLS HER HAIR

"I am going back in a week," she answered dejectedly as she suspected his reasons for asking were so he could be free of his obligation to keep Mary placated by dancing with her.

About that time, Harry Henderson walked by and gave Warren a wink and a smile as he said, "Good dutiful boy."

Warren began to have an idea germinate in his head. Hey, this was an unsophisticated, frumpy girl who had a fairly pretty face and desperately longed for his attention. Why not try out a few of his manipulative girl bait lines on her to see if they might work? Then he could spring the better ones on girls in whom he was really interested. Yeah, why waste his time? Why not make this forced interlude productive?

He turned, put on an air of intense masculinity, looked deeply and longingly into her eyes and said with what appeared to be great passion and

J. Wayne Frye

conviction, "My goodness you've got an awfully kissable mouth Letty."

That remark was like a bomb blast in a deserted area. It seemed to bounce, reverberated and dance about with deviltry of purpose. Letty instinctively lowered her head and fidgeted in her seat. She turned an ungraceful red and began to breathe heavily as she let out a faint, slow sigh. No one had ever made such a remark to her before. Oh my, she thought. What am I to do?

Without thinking, she said, "You presumptuous jerk," and winced a bit, sit up straighter and cocked her head in defiance. However, she secretly liked it. She let out a little grin that proved it.

There is nothing inherently wrong in a man complimenting a woman, as long as it is within the bounds of probity. Warren felt he was just being complimentary, even though he did have an ulterior motive. Why he thought did she react that way? He wasn't a jerk. He was just a man who was complimenting a woman on her lips. What was wrong with that?

Speaking of lips, back in Cavite, Philippines, Lynton was busy conversing on the internet with a man to whom she had never sent a picture. She was pleasantly surprised at his niceness. In fact, he had told her when they were corresponding by e-mail to not worry about a picture, as he was more interested in her inner beauty than her outer beauty. However, when he first gazed upon her on the internet video chat, he simply could not believe how beautiful she was, and wondered why she would have anything to do with a much older man who had left his good looks behind him about ten years ago. Still, for some reason, she was attracted to him.

And how he was titillated by her incredible puffy, succulent, alluring lips. He timidly mentioned to her how beautiful her lips were and how he would love to kiss them someday. Unlike Letty, Lynton smiled and thanked him for the compliment. She was a woman with great poise and charm who welcomed a compliment from a man. This would be the first of many compliments from a man who truly appreciated Lynton, not just for her beauty but also for her depth of character.

Back in Asheboro, the erstwhile Warren was trying to recover from a misstep in his continental charm offensive. Warren was annoyed as he was not accustomed to having a remark like the one about Letty's mouth considered inappropriate. He ignored what she had said and seemed charitable as he switched the topic. "Edward Bolton and Ethel Everett are sitting out the dancing as usual."

This kind of talk was more suited to Letty's conversing abilities, but a faint regret mingled with her relief as the subject changed, because no man had ever talked to her about kissable mouths, but she knew that they talked in some such way to other girls. Yeah, she was offended and flattered at the same time. Why she thought? Why am I flattered by an inappropriate comment about my mouth? It had actually made her heart beat faster and it was just now settling down.

"Oh, yes," she said, and laughed coyly. "I hear they come from poor families. Why do they let them in?"

Warren, who was somewhat less arrogant about wealth than his blueblood friends, did not appreciate the comment, because Edward was a close friend of his brother's, and anyway he considered it bad form to sneer at people for not having money. But perhaps he thought Letty had had no intention of sneering at them. Maybe she was merely nervous and trying to make conversation, trying to fit in to Asheboro's high society. Hey, it wasn't easy for a wallflower like her.

The evening wore on and the uncomfortable feelings between the two slightly diminished. When

LYNTON CURLS HER HAIR

Mary and Letty reached home at half after midnight they said good night at the top of the spiral staircase that wound opulently upward as it reached the fabulously ornate landing that was the size of many people's homes. Though cousins, they were not particularly close. As a matter of fact, Mary had no real close female friends, as she preferred male friends. Letty, on the contrary, all through this parent-arranged visit had rather longed to exchange those confidences flavoured with giggles and tears that she considered an indispensable factor in all feminine intercourse. But in this respect she found Mary rather cold. In fact, she felt somehow the same difficulty in talking to her that she had talking to men. Mary never giggled, was never frightened, seldom embarrassed, and in fact had very few of the qualities which Letty considered normal for a female.

As Letty meticulously prepared for bed, while using her electric toothbrush, she stared into the bathroom mirror and wondered why men did not favour her with attention. Ironically, as she stared at her wild hair, it never occurred to her that might be one of the reasons. After all, her family was fabulously wealthy, even more so than Mary's. That, alone, she thought, should be reason for men to be interested. After all, at 21, she was a good catch, if for no other reason, than her family's social status and immense wealth. She contemplated whether or not she should go to Mary and ask her to provide some solid womanly guidance on the situation.

Letty felt a vague misery about the situation and may have felt worse if she had known that it was Mary's intervention that made it possible for her to have any attention from men. Why she thought did other girls get so much attention from men? She attributed it to something subtly unscrupulous in those girls. It had never worried her before, and she always assured herself that other women cheapened themselves by making themselves so readily available to men.

LYNTON CURLS HER HAIR

Lynton, on the other hand, rarely felt cheapened by the attention of men, although she never actively sought it. In fact, when she met Wayne, she had only had two serious relationships, and one of them was just passing fancy more than anything else, as it had occurred in her older adolescence and lasted only a few months. The second was much more serious and she wound up living with the man for six years before infidelity on his part led to a rather furious break-up. She was a lady, but she was also a lady who did not tolerate infidelity from a lover.

Wayne actually found it humorous that such a demure, unassuming, reticent young woman could be so upset that when she caught her boyfriend in bed with another woman she would hit him. That led him to say to Lynton, "Hey, I will never cheat on you, because I am afraid of you."

Are there reasons why things like this happen? Does fate play an active role in the order of our lives? Well, Lynton was a woman who believed, unlike Letty, that there was a reason things happened the way they do. She felt that catching her boyfriend cheating turned out to be positive eventually. She told Wayne, "It happened, because I was destined to meet you. If I had not caught him cheating, that would not have happened, and your wife ran off with another man for the same reason. You would not have met me otherwise. Fate is a hopeful hunter."

Lynton's perceptiveness was far beyond that of Letty, who saw things as they were and assumed in stoic fashion that what one saw on the surface was the totality; whereas, Lynton understood that if you looked beneath the surface you could find the inherent good or the implicit evil of each individual. A cursory surveillance of the individual rarely revealed the inner most light of exceptionality or the darkness of the villainy.

Lynton was a woman who knew that physical beauty would fade with time, but that the inner beauty would last forever. To her, the physical was too often a façade that hid the ugliness while the true worth was beneath the surface where the authentic foundation of a person lay. Through her trials she had found that many times if you dug beneath the surface you could find the seeds of either discontent or the seeds of nourishment. The rose is a hardy flower, because its root system goes deep beneath the soil in search of sustenance to keep the vibrancy that makes it so valuable in the scheme of things. It refuses to die, because it has a solid foundation beneath the surface. So, a solid foundation is necessary for true beauty to break through to the surface of possibilities.

As she turned out the light in the bathroom, Letty on an impulse decided to go in and chat for a moment with her Aunt Martha since Mary simply wasn't interested in an exploration of anything of substance. Her soft slippers bore her noiselessly down the carpeted hall, but hearing voices inside she stopped near the slightly ajar door. Then she caught her own name, and without any definite intention of eavesdropping, she lingered and the thread of the conversation going on inside pierced her consciousness sharply as if it had been drawn through with a needle.

"She's absolutely totally hopeless!" It was Mary's voice. "Oh, I know what you're going to say! So many people have told you how she is from a wealthy family and just needs some coaching and a bit more refinement. I am telling you she simply is too backwards to ever attract a man. She is actually beyond hopeless. She is pitiful."

Aunt Martha, seemingly irritated, showed her frustration as she said, "It is your duty to teach her, not ridicule her."

Sighing, Mary said, "I have done my best. I've been polite and I've made men dance with her, but they just won't stand being bored. She has no social grace at all. How can someone from such a socially prominent family be so utterly incompetent in all the mannerisms of refinement? It is an abomination the way she acts."

Martha, getting a bit perturbed said, "Well, she will be going home in a week, so it will be a moot point. Surely after all this time, one more week is tolerable."

"Are you kidding, I can not endure bolstering her ego any longer. I am sick of it. I've even tried to drop hints about clothes and things, and she's been furious and given me the funniest looks. Oh, and that God-awful hair of hers. She's sensitive enough to know she's not getting the attention of men, but I'll bet she consoles herself by thinking that she's very virtuous and that I'm too promiscuous and fickle in my social graces. All unpopular girls think that way. Sour grapes! I'll bet she'd give ten years of her life and her European education to have three or four men in love with her and be cut in on every dance."

LYNTON CURLS HER HAIR

"It seems to me," interrupted Martha rather wearily, "that you ought to be able to do something for her, one final act to propel her into doing something dramatic to change her outlook on things, something to boost her confidence. You are her cousin, give her some help."

"Are you kidding? I've never heard her say anything to a boy except that it's hot or the floor's crowded or that she went to school in Switzerland. Sometimes she asks them what kind of car they have and tells them the kind she has. She even asks them if they like chicken nuggets. She is hopeless. I tell you, hopeless."

Martha, thinking contemplatively, after a long silence, said, "All I know is that other girls not half so sweet and attractive get partners at those country club dances in that high-toned place on the hill. Amanda Fox, for instance, is stout and loud, and her mother is distinctly common. Alice Dorman is so thin this year that she looks like she could use a bracelet as a hula hoop, but they all still get plenty of interest from men."

"But, mother," objected Mary impatiently, "Amanda is cheerful and awfully witty, and Alice is a marvellous dancer. They may not be perfect physical specimens, but they have some personality. Letty has absolutely zilch when it comes to personality."

Now, it is easy to point the finger of condemnation at people of colour, and Mary knew that Letty had a great grandmother who was American Indian, so prejudice suddenly reared its ugly head as Mary blurted out, "I think it's that crazy Indian blood in her. Maybe she should go to a reservation where everyone is uncouth like her. She would fit right in with people who have no social grace. Besides, Indian women all sit around and say nothing. Letty would be good at that, because when she says something it is a disaster. She'd be much better off just keeping her mouth shut."

LYNTON CURLS HER HAIR

"Don't let this discussion deteriorate into ethnic attacks darling. Go to bed and just think about it. Frankly, I am a bit disappointed in you. Just because you come from wealth and are white doesn't give you the right to disparage minorities. Go to bed and think about doing the right thing."

Knowing Mary was on her way out, Letty slipped into the library and hid behind the open door just as Mary walked back to her room muttering something under her breath that was undetectable to Letty. Hanging her head and contemplating the contempt for her displayed by Mary, Letty felt like crying but vowed to not do so out of determination to not allow her emotions to get the best of her. O.K., so Mary was a bitch. Hey, she already knew that. She even knew Mary resented having to find her guys to dance with. So, what she said was already evident. It was just that she had not come out and voiced it. Anyway thought Letty, most of what she said was the truth. I just as well face the fact that I am a total disaster. I am a walking, talking loser with no hope.

J. Wayne Frye

CHAPTER 4

WITHOUT YOU, I AM NOTHING

While Mary was having breakfast the next day, Letty came into the room with a scowl on her face, unceremoniously sat down opposite her, stared intently over and let out a long sigh. As she did, Mary grimaced, but decided some civility was in order, so she ignored her for a second seeming to be searching for words. Letty just sat with a scowl on her face. She was in a fowl mood, but more than anything she wanted help in becoming more appealing to men.

LYNTON CURLS HER HAIR

"What's shaking girl?" inquired Mary, rather puzzled.

Letty sat and continued to stare, looking ready to explode like a stick of dynamite with a short fuse. "I heard what you said about me to your mother last night."

Mary was shocked, but was measured and matter of fact in her reply, "Where were you?"

"In the hall; I didn't mean to listen at first, but I couldn't help myself."

After a cowing look of contempt, Mary lowered her head to avoid looking directly at Letty and was stoically silent with a mild tinge of shame.

"I guess I'd better go back home today, if I'm such a nuisance and a handicap in your social life." Letty's lower lip was trembling and she was on the verge of crying. "I've tried to be nice, and I've been

J. Wayne Frye

first made to feel unwelcome and then second insulted behind my back."

Mary lifted her head, rubbed her right hand across her forehead and just couldn't find words. All her smoothness, manipulative and communicative skills seemed to have dissipated.

Letty continued, "I'm in your way. I am a drag on your social life. I'm a drag on you. Your friends detest me." She paused, and then remembered another one of her grievances. "Of course, I will freely admit being jealous of you. You are so skilled in social graces, and men, even women, seem to flock around you. Your personality and confident manner put you in good steed with everyone. Being around you is exciting, and being around me is the pits."

"No, that is not entirely true," murmured Mary.

"What" replied, a discordant sounding Letty.

"You aren't that bad. I am just being judgmental and I have approached you in an inappropriate manner at times I suppose," said Mary with a tone of contriteness that seemed a bit sincere, though not entirely. "I should have been nicer I suppose looking back at things. I thought pawning you off on boys was all that was required of me. I have treated you abysmally, but frankly I did not realize it until now."

Then, Mary said, "When do you want to go?"

Surprised, Letty replied, "What?"

"You said you wanted to go home. When did you want to go, right now? I could help you pack your bags of you are serious. There is a train leaves at 4:00 o'clock today."

Perturbed at what she perceived as a lack of concern, Letty said "Do you think that was a very nice thing to say?"

J. Wayne Frye

"I wasn't trying to be nice, Letty." Then after a pause, she continued, "So, when do you want to go?"

Still shocked by Mary's apparent lack of remorse for the cruelty she had perpetrated, all Letty could let out as tears formed in her eyes was, "Oh, oh my!"

Mary, seemingly out of character, because despite her many flaws, she was generally exceedingly nice to people for manipulative reasons, said, "Hey, you did say you were going."

"Yes, but ——"

"Oh, you were only bluffing, then! You actually had no plans to go after all, a bluff, just a bluff," interjected Mary.

They stared at each other across the breakfast-table for a moment. Misty waves of passion and disgust were passing before Letty's eyes, while Mary's face was stolid and hard, almost as if she was totally unconcerned with how much she was hurting Letty.

Once again, she blurted out, "So, you were only bluffing. You have no intention of leaving, then?

Letty burst into uncontrollable tears as she buried her head in her hands.

"You are my cousin," cried Letty, and through sobs she continued, "I came here because I like you. I thought I could learn something about the social graces from you. If I go home, my mother will be upset with me, say that I don't know how to act around other people and that I am socially inept."

Then, Mary's cruelty seemed to harden when it came to Letty leaving. "Then I'll give you some money. You can get yourself a nice hotel in town – absolutely no problem."

J. Wayne Frye

LYNTON CURLS HER HAIR

It was more than Letty could take. She jumped up, still sobbing and literally ran out of the room as Mary shrugged her shoulders and let out a disgusted sigh.

Now, let's contrast this to the way Lynton's friend Ingrid treated her when Lynton faced a crisis of confidence. As a 16 year old, Lynton was confronted with a severe family dilemma when her mother and father split up. It is not the purpose of this book to explore what happened in detail, but suffice it to say it was no trivial matter.

Lynton came home from school one day and all her belongings were out in the street. The family home she had been staying in by herself so she could finish high school had been sold, and no provisions were made for the young woman who stood on the streets bewildered and confused.

This young, fragile, mild-mannered, demure adolescent was desperate and did not know where to turn. However, true friendship can turn lambs into lions. When you are alone and the clouds of despair darken your existence that is when you can really count your friends. It is the trials of life that makes us realize that a person who stands by us and tries to lighten our burdens is the very essence of a friend; Lynton had that in a young woman named Ingrid.

On that horrible day, Ingrid came upon Lynton and saw her standing in the street with a look of deep despair on her face. After an explanation from Lynton, she put her arms around her shoulders and said, "Grab your things and come home with me."

Thus began a friendship totally dissimilar to that shared by Mary and Letty. It was a mutually devoted friendship that would endure a lifetime. Fortunately, Ingrid had a sympathetic mother who willingly welcomed Lynton into her home, and thus began a formative time in Lynton's life, when she was fortunate enough to have sustenance and a roof over her head, but still she had to learn to fend for herself. Many people would have been weakened by despair like that suffered by the young woman, but it actually made Lynton stronger, and more determined. She refused to give into melancholy, despondency and hopelessness. She was a woman of strong will and character who fortunately had a loyal friend in Ingrid who would always be dependable and never resort to displaying the cruelty manifested by Mary. This friendship endured through the years. Even when Lynton found Wayne and fell in love with him, one of her first acts was to share details of the romance with Ingrid, let her meet Wayne and get her opinion of him, as she valued her counsel.

Now, let us go back to what was occurring in Mary's home, where Mary had sequestered herself in the library. She sat at the computer, composing a letter in haste. She was almost livid over the affair.

An hour later, while Mary was in the library absorbed in composing, Letty reappeared, very red-eyed, but consciously calm. She cast no glance at Mary but took a book at random from the shelf and sat down as if to read. Mary seemed absorbed in her letter and continued composing. When the clock showed noon, Letty closed her book with a snap. "I suppose I'd better get my railroad ticket," she said with an air of disdain.

She regretted saying that, because she had been practicing a demonstrative speech upstairs. My goodness she thought – I certainly blew it. I was all set to wow her with my incredible rhetoric, and all I do is sound acquiescent to her suggestions to get out of town. She had planned to urge her to be more reasonable, more caring, more accommodating and more understanding.

"Just wait till I finish this e-mail," said Mary, seemingly disinterested and unconcerned, not even looking up from the computer as she pounded away frantically on the keyboard. "I want to get it off right away."

J. Wayne Frye

LYNTON CURLS HER HAIR

After another minute, during which Mary laboriously continued to pound the keyboard, she turned round and matter-of-factly said, "at your service. Now, let me know how I can help you my dear."

"Do you want me to go home," said Letty, almost pleading, and hating herself for stooping so low before an obviously uncaring, totally repugnant Mary.

"Well," said Mary, contemplatively, "I suppose if you're not having a good time you'd better go. No use being miserable."

Still thoroughly shocked by her apparent unconcern, Letty replied, "Don't you have any common decency?"

With an air of aloofness and unconcern, Mary said, "Come on, show a little class and style, Letty. You said you wanted to go."

"How can you be so cold hearted and callous, Mary?"

"According to my mother, you are just like your own mother, who was also a social pariah as are you," callously replied Mary.

"Mary, please do not make disparaging remarks about my dear mother," said a very deeply offended Letty.

Mary laughed in an exceedingly sarcastic manner. "I don't think there is anything wrong in stating facts."

Letty, almost bowing her head, said, "Anyway, that is off the subject. Do you think you have been very kind to me?"

"Hey, I have worked diligently to get boys to pay some attention to you, but you always blow it. You have no social poise whatsoever. I have done my best. Hey, you aren't very easy material to work with."

A pensive, forlorn Letty with reddening eyes, said, "I think you are acting abominably. I am sorry I can't live up to your standards. I can't believe you are being so mean.

"Please," beseeched Mary, who was in no mood to let up. "Girls like you are colourless, boring and will never conquer you inferior abilities to attract men. Some women just don't have it, and believe me; you don't have it – no way, no how, not now, not ever. What a blow it must be to realize how inadequate you are when it comes to attracting men. You are pathetic."

Her mouth hanging wide open, Letty could not believe the cruelties that were emanating from the mouth of her cousin. She sat bewildered, unable to even utter a word, as she looked in total bewilderment at Mary.

The vindictiveness simply would not let up. "You are a whining mouse of a woman with no backbone, no ability to tackle even the most fundamental of the social graces. There's some excuse for an ugly girl whining. If I'd been irretrievably ugly I'd never have forgiven my parents for bringing me into the world. But you're starting life without any handicap. You could be beautiful if you'd do something with that God awful hair." Then she turned off the computer, nonchalantly waved her wrist at Letty and continued. "If you expect me to weep with you you'll be disappointed. Go or stay, just as you like. You see, I am past caring what you do."

Ironically, Mary's e-mail was to a pen pal in the Philippines with whom she had developed a friendly relationship. As Mary's e-mail was making its way through the Ethernet to that person, Lynton and Wayne's budding romance was in full bloom as he had arrived in the Philippines to court her in person.

LYNTON CURLS HER HAIR

Now, this story is not about the romance between Lynton and Wayne, as that is the subject for another book, but it is imperative that there be some rudimentary knowledge of the romance in order to understand the significance of something that occurs later between these two lovers that will actually be related to what is going to happen to Letty in Asheboro, North Carolina. Although the distance between Cavite, Philippines and Asheboro, North Carolina is over 14,000 kilometres, what occurred in those two places almost simultaneously is what this unique story is all about. Consequently, it is imperative that the readers have some perspective on what took place between these two lovers for thorough comprehension.

Their meeting at the Manila Airport was filled with emotion for both of them as they greeted each other with no trepidation since they felt like they genuinely already knew each other intimately. As they made their way in a family van to Lynton's home, they gently kissed one another and Wayne slipped a ring on her hand. It was not an expensive diamond, but rather a practical expression of his love for her, and his intention to make her his partner for the time he had left on the earth. As they rode through the teeming streets of metropolitan Manila, they held hands, and the diminutive Lynton placed her head gently on the much larger Wayne's left shoulder. He sighed and said, "You are more beautiful than I ever imagined. You are a beacon of light that shines in the darkness of my despair and lights up my life with hope, anticipation and confidence in a future where love makes all things possible."

Lynton seemed to melt into his arms, blending her soul into his as she said, "I am yours forever."

That afternoon, as they rode together oblivious to everything around them, the two of them began to realize that the affection they developed on line for one another was much more than just a passing fancy. Theirs was a genuine May-December romance in the vein of Charlie Chaplin and Oona O'Neill. Wayne could never understand how Lynton could be so much in love with a man who had passed his prime in looks, vitality and virility, but his thinking skirted the inner most reaches of a woman who thought with her heart, and was able to see within Wayne that which was not apparent to anyone who did not look deep within her and comprehend what she had been looking for in a man all her life. Despite Wayne's inability to see the good, kind, non-judgmental depth of his own character, Lynton was able to recognize and ferret out that which he seemed oblivious to, because her depth of love for him was based upon that which was not on the surface, but lay deep within the psyche of a man who had captured the heart of an extraordinary woman.

Over the next few weeks Lynton and Wayne's love for one another developed methodically, slowly and in deep intensity as they found a natural simpatico that drew them ever closer into a web of affection and love that seemed to engross and consume them. A dedicated devotion to one another's welfare made them ever cognizant of how it seemed that fate had intervened in both their lives to bring them together in a unification of passion, tenderness and warmth.

One cannot love Lynton without also loving her two best friends Ingrid and Channa. While Wayne was getting acquainted with these two lovely ladies, and begin to appreciate that even in her friends, Lynton reflected that which was deeply representative of her depth of character, back in Asheboro, Mary and Letty were reaching a crossroads in a developing scenario that would alter Letty's life and lead to catastrophe.

Going out for a day of frivolities with two different men, Mary's Saturday afternoon trysts had been part of her life since she was a teenager. When she returned late in the afternoon she found Letty with a strangely set face waiting for her in her bedroom. Letty had a look of determination on her face as she said, "I have decided that maybe you are correct about things. You have a crude, mean way of putting it, but you may be right about me. I suppose I am most of the things you say I am. So, though you did it in mean fashion, I think maybe I should heed your counsel."

Mary, admiring herself in the mirror, could not believe what Letty was saying. "Do you mean it?"

"Yes."

"So, you want me to help you I suppose? You now realize that I have superior knowledge in male-female relationships?"

"If what you suggest does not alter my moral perspective, yes."

Mary, almost gloating about the power she was being offered by Letty, replied in a determined fashion, "So, I tell you what to wear, what to say, what to do, how to act in absolutely every way. You will put yourself in the hands of the master then?"

"Yes, yes."

Mary, thoroughly enjoying her power, said, "Everything I ask of you, without question, right? I tell you to boldly prance down Main Street in your pyjamas singing Dixie, carrying a confederate flag and you will do it?

"Yes, except for the flag. Remember, I said to the limits of my moral fibre Mary. I could not carry that flag, because it represents years of suppression for African-Americans. I would prance down the street though and sing Dixie, yes."

"O.K. girl. I'll accept those caveats," replied Mary, who was feeling somewhat exhilarated over having brought Letty into her lair of manipulative control.

LYNTON CURLS HER HAIR

"Great, so where do we begin?"

"First you have no ease of manner. Why? Because you're never sure about your personal appearance. I mean look at yourself objectively. When a girl feels that she's perfectly groomed and dressed she can forget that part of her. That's charm. The more parts of yourself you can afford to forget the more charm you have."

Sort of surveying herself up and down as she talked, Letty said, "So, I don't look very good? I can understand that, I suppose."

"Girl, you look O.K., but you need to be stunning. I am going to show you how to be gorgeous."

Hanging her head a bit, Letty, almost in a whisper, said, "Stunning? That is a pretty tall order for a wallflower like me. I know it is easy for you, but me? I am not so sure. I have none of your skills remember."

LYNTON CURLS HER HAIR

"Look, you are half-way there, because you are actually a pretty girl. What you need is just a touch of elegance. You need to develop an air of confidence about you. You can be diminutive in size but with self-confidence you seem statuesque even at a small height. Self-confidence makes you appear taller. Also remember that no matter what you do, let that sophistication show. Men love sophistication, especially those who lack it themselves. Somehow it inflates their egos to have a beautiful, sophisticated woman on their arm. Men are such ninnies."

How ironic that as Mary was talking about self-confidence, Wayne was telling Lynton much to her delight, as they sit in a beauty salon in Cavite, that she was a woman of infinite charm, beauty and so self-confident.

What Lynton said to Wayne that day would forever endear her to him. Letting that provocative, alluring, gorgeous, captivating smile slowly creep

J. Wayne Frye

across her lips as her glistening white teeth sparkled in the sunlight that danced through the plate glass window, she said, "I have confidence because of you. You make me feel beautiful and alluring with your words."

How true that statement is, because words can be used to build people up or to tear them down. Unfortunately, they too often are used to tear people down. Lynton had, for a variety of reasons during her lifetime, suffered at the hands of those who were prejudiced against people who dared to be a be different. The world is filled with those who think that anyone who does not adhere to the norm is somehow unworthy of respect and acceptance. Sexual orientation, social status, wealth, education, physical looks are often used as measures of worth when true worth should be measured by a person's character. Lynton was a woman who refused to bow before bigotry and indifference. She avoided almost all controversy when people were cruel and indifferent toward her by simply saying, "That is their problem, and I won't let them pull me down to their level."

Each passing day was a delight to these two, because they were forming a bond of love that would grow, prosper and endure. All those about them could sense a radiant glow of affection that seemed to emanate deep from within Wayne and Lynton and flow like a babbling brook over smooth rocks. These two were profoundly in love.

As they left the salon that day, Lynton would say something to Wayne that would ultimately lead to an event that would, for Lynton, make her realize that this was a man whose love for her was beyond reproach. She would conclusively comprehend that one act of affection can solidify that which you think is true but of which you are not 100% sure, by bringing to the surface from deep within the realization that one person, one event, one solitary act can make you understand just how much one person can love another.

LYNTON CURLS HER HAIR

What was it she said? It seemed innocuous at the time, but as she and Wayne walked arm-in-arm through the teeming streets of Dasmarinas City, Lynton looked at a girl with beautiful curly hair, reached up and stroked her own straight hair and said, "I wish I could get my hair done to make it curly like that. It is just too expensive, though."

Wayne said nothing in reply, only looked at her and smiled, but like a family heirloom tucked away in some safe place, he let that comment slowly find a corner of his mind where it would lie dormant until resurrected with love and passion. He recalled something he had once read: *yesterday is but today's memory and tomorrow is today's dream.* And Wayne dreamed of tomorrow with Lynton. Tomorrow was his hope for salvation in the deep recesses of a heart filled with love.

Wayne was a man who had a heart that never hardened, a temper that never flared and a touch that was appreciated and revered by Lynton as it made her feel the gentle love that flowed from deep within a man who had captured her heart at a time when she had almost given up on love. When the gentle night came, it was softened and hued with soft passion from Wayne who had reserved in his heart a place for stars of delight to sparkle with love for Lynton. He made her the face of heaven in his eyes and bowed in glorious homage to she whom he adored above all others.

As they strolled the streets, the sun slowly disappeared and the stars began to twinkle. Wayne stopped, stood and pointed his fingers as if counting the stars. Lynton said, "What are you doing?"

"I am counting. In the arithmetic of love, one plus one equals everything and two minus one equals nothing." Then he placed his arms around her and continued, "Without you I am nothing."

CHAPTER 5

UNTIL MY LAST BREATH

There are times when one can sense the coming doom. As Mary and Letty were discussing how to make Letty appear more appealing to men, the sun was shining brightly as they sit at the breakfast table. The warm morning rays of sunshine seemed to dance about the table, reflecting all about the room, lighting it with hope and anticipation that tomorrow would offer hope and renewal. That hope was what Letty was looking for in a world that she seemed to be closing in on her.

LYNTON CURLS HER HAIR

Despite the brightness, there was a dark cloud on the horizon, moving slowly toward the sun as Mary said, "Your black and lustrous eyebrows are beautiful if you'd take care of them just a little better. Brush them several times a day. It helps flatten them and makes them more alluring."

Letty raised the brows in question and said, "You mean men actually look at your eyebrows?"

Shaking her head, Mary replied, "Girl, men are lechers. They look at everything."

Wow, you are so perceptive and knowledgeable about men."

Smiling, Mary replied, "You are right about that. I have been studying them for years, and I know all the tricks to use. It is easy to manipulate men. They are asking for it. They just don't know it, but they are begging for a woman to take control. I have never met a man I couldn't control."

LYNTON CURLS HER HAIR

Letty leaned forward slightly and said, "Bet I am not dancing right with them either am I?"

"Dancing my dear Letty is the way to drive a man crazy with desire. Don't dance straight like you do. Lean over on the man and sort of fall into his arms. Let out a little sigh on occasion, as if you are fawning over his manliness. Act the part of a dainty little thing that needs a big strong man to wrap her in his arms and protect her."

Now Letty was really interested. Each word spoken by Mary seemed to be a droplet of wisdom. It was as if Mary was providing the sweetener for Letty's cup of knowledge about men. It was filling up, and the swizzle stick to stir it with was Mary's understanding of the art of being seductive.

"You have got to learn to be nice to men who are just like ripe apples on a tree. You can pick and choose the ripest, tastiest ones. You look as if you'd faint with embarrassment at any breech of probity and you act like you are a dainty creature who needs a man to protect you. Many of the best prospects are men too shy to talk. They love a woman who brings out their natural nature to be protective. Drop something for them to gallantly pick up, or mutter something about how polite they are or how you like their necktie. Once you break the ice, they will start talking with ease."

Letty was now hanging on every word, mesmerized by Mary's knowledge of the courting game. And Mary was enjoying her role as teacher of the seductive arts. She continued as if she was Aristotle in ancient Greece pontificating to eager students. "Clumsy boys are the best dancing practice. If you can follow them and still look graceful you can traverse a mine field in a battle zone and come out unscathed."

Mary was so wound up that she was like a tank rambling though a battlefield, mowing down everything its path, as her words were now flowing like a machine gun spitting out bullets. "If you go to a dance and really amuse, say, three guys that dance with you; if you talk so well to them that they forget they're stuck with you, you've done something. They'll come back next time and gradually so many will dance with you that the more desirable men will start to think this girl must be special."

An ecstatic Letty interjected, "Yeah, I begin to see."

"Of course you do. You are listening to the master. Poise and charm are within striking distance for you now, Letty. You'll wake up some morning knowing you've attained it and men will know it too. Then you will, like me, know that all this is just an artful game where those with the knowledge are always at the head of the class."

Then came the pièce de résistance from the fountain of knowledge offered by Mary. It would be the crown jewel of advice.

LYNTON CURLS HER HAIR

Mary dropped her voice a bit and said, "I have given you the keys to make yourself every bit as magnetically enticing as I am, but there is one thing left that you must do. Without it, you will only be partially successful. Do this and you will be more tantalizing than you ever dreamed possible."

Letty was enthralled and sat staring, waiting with great anticipation for the final piece of the puzzle to be put in place. Mary, with egotistical self-confidence that she was the master of the art of beguiling men, let a smile slowly creep across her face and said, "That hair. That abdominal wild hair that is all over the place must go. Go to a beauty salon and get it styled. Have it straighten just a bit, but keep the curls, because fluffy full hair is very seductive to men. Just get that awful mop trimmed a bit. That is all. It is an absolute must."

Letty made no answer but gazed pensively at the window where her reflection made her realize just how horrible her hair looked. She said, "Ugh."

J. Wayne Frye

LYNTON CURLS HER HAIR

As both girls looked at the reflection in the large bay kitchen window, the breakfast room nook began to darken as that lone cloud covered the sun, moving across the light and blacking it out. A slight breeze began to blow outside and the leaves rustled against the windowpane, making a hideous scratching noise. Little did either of them know that it was an ill wind of despair blowing into their lives?

Now, this book is entitled *Lynton Curls Her Hair*, so the logical question from the reader would be why we are talking about Letty's hair? The answer lies a bit beneath the surface, as both women are headed toward a rendezvous with destiny, but two very different destinies based upon two distinct personalities and two uniquely different women from divergent backgrounds.

Wayne and Lynton's romance continued unabated, and Lynton put her comment about her hair in the back recesses of a mind that was so preoccupied with love nothing else seemed to matter. However, Wayne did not put it in the back of his mind. Like he did with most things in his life, there would be a distinct, detailed, well-formulated plan. It was a plan based upon the love he had for this extraordinary woman. It would be held in abeyance for a while, and then at the right moment, he would use it to solidify his devotion to Lynton. It would be a method to make her realize just how deeply he loved her. Wayne was not a religious man, but he was a student of the Bible, having read it from cover to cover many times in his life. He recalled a line from Ecclesiastes: *To every thing there is a season, and a time to every purpose under the heaven.* Yes, at that moment when she mentioned she wanted curly hair, Wayne, so much in love and wanting to prove to her how much she was loved by him, filed that comment away and started formulating a plan that would solidify in Lynton's mind just how much she was adored by a man old enough to be her father, but still able to feel like a teenager in love. There would definitely be a season in the future when Wayne, who already knew the purpose, would make her realize just how much he adored her by one act of love he would perform that would bring tears of joy to her eyes.

Love can happen in an instance. Or, it can happen gradually, grow and germinate over a period of time. It can occur at the most inopportune times. It can come like a thunderbolt from the sky striking with the precision of a laser, or it can be like a phantom slipping up unexpectedly in the night and taking hold of you. There is no real pattern to love. It is often as unexpected as a snowstorm in the middle of June. Yet, Wayne and Lynton had already prepared themselves for love, because they knew one another so well before they met in person that it was no shock when they had their first soft kiss, held hands as they walked through the airport parking lot and sit beside one another in a van and longingly stared at one another in anticipation of a few weeks where they would see their love grow gradually and solidify.

LYNTON CURLS HER HAIR

While visiting, Wayne noticed that Lynton was often complaining of a backache, and one day at her home Wayne walked into her bedroom as she was receiving a massage to relieve her pain in another room. He lay down on the mattress and instantly knew why she was having back trouble. It was so thin and worn that basically she was sleeping on the hard plywood that was beneath it. Now most people get frivolous gifts on their birthdays, Valentines Day and Christmas. Wayne, ever practical, knew that Lynton's birthday was only a week away, so why not surprise her with the perfect and most practical gift – a mattress.

It was a gift that touched Lynton deeply and made her realize that Wayne was not the typical boyfriend who lavished you with impractical gifts to dazzle you. He had already proven that when he showed up at the airport with a very unusual gift. He had been so captivated by her alluring smile and white teeth that he brought her an electric toothbrush. She fought back laughter but realized his gifts were truly unique, as this was a man who did not ascribe to superficiality or impracticality. Yet, Wayne's penchant for the practical would be a cover for the impractical act that would occur a month or so later, an impractical act that would seem out of character, but make Lynton realize this was a man who genuinely loved her beyond her wildest dreams. There is love and then there is deep, abiding love. The later was what she would discover Wayne had for her.

Letty had made an appointment at the beauty salon for the following Friday to have her hair cut, styled and meticulously curled. However, that Wednesday there was a dinner-dance at the country club. She did the best she could with her hair, and it was not quiet as wild, but was still less than stellar in appearance. When the guests strolled in she was seated next to a most desirable bachelor on one side, Bill Steadman, and on the other side, Chuck Pauley, someone she considered a bit lacklustre based upon her new enlightenment courtesy of Mary.

LYNTON CURLS HER HAIR

Ready to play the game the way Mary taught her, she decided to practice a little vamping on Chuck Pauley as she assumed she should start with someone a little less sophisticated than Bill Steadman. She very coyly turned toward him and said, "Chuck, do you think I should get my hair trimmed and naturally curled? I am giving it consideration but need the opinion of a wise man about it."

"Why?"

"Because I'm considering it as a way of attracting more attention and you are sort of a man-of-the world. What do you think? Would it get the attention of a sophisticated man like you?"

Chuck, feeling flattered, puffed out his chest and said, "I don't know a lot about females' hair, but I do think you might benefit from a little different style. Don't get me wrong. You look O.K. now, but a different style might suit you better."

LYNTON CURLS HER HAIR

Letty decided to really poor it on thick, to go all the way with her newfound ability to vamp men. "I want to be a society vampire and devour handsome men like you with my charm and looks. I want to nibble on your neck. "

Feeling even more self-assured and cocky since a woman was complementing him; Chuck again puffed out his chest and sighed as if in deep thought about the subject. "Well, as a man who knows a bit about women, I would say you would improve your chances of successfully wooing men with a different hair style."

"Oh my," a fawning Letty replied, "you are so knowledgeable and wise Chuck." Her fake sincerity seemed genuine as she continued, "Receiving wise counsel from a sophisticated ladies man like you is so helpful."

As she blinked her eyes at him, Chuck replied rather arrogantly, "Glad to help."

LYNTON CURLS HER HAIR

"So I've decided thanks to your wise counsel," she continued, her voice rising slightly, "that I'm going down to the salon and get it done. She noticed that she had been so effective that the people near her had paused in their conversation and were listening; and then, she got even bolder. "Of course I'm charging admission, but if you'll all come down and encourage me I'll issue passes for the inside seats."

There was raucous laughter from all, and Bill Steadman leaned over and whispered in her ear, "I'll take a box-seat right now. How much is the admission charge. Whatever it is, I'll pay the price, because it will be worth it."

She was really working it now, and feeling a sense of exhilaration. She turned to him, making sure her lips were close to his as she said, "My goodness, you are an eager beaver aren't you? Why I may just let you sit in the chair with me if you are a really good boy."

94 J. Wayne Frye

LYNTON CURLS HER HAIR

A titillated Bill excitedly interjected, "You are teasing me."

Letty was now feeling like a master manipulator of men, even before she had her hair done. "Oh Bill, I would never tease a darling man like you, but I either have to amuse people or be a wallflower. Now, I don't think being a wallflower is any fun."

She had not even had her hair done yet, but it had already changed her personality just thinking about it. She leaned across the table a bit and winked at Danny Crutchen. She made a slight motion with her head and he got the cue. He shouted, "Let's dance Letty."

The rest of the night was spent dancing and vamping man after man, each one of them eager to know what she would look like in her new hairstyle as Letty kept talking about it, building it up like it was an event of monumental proportions. The change in her personality caused a buzz.

LYNTON CURLS HER HAIR

The next day as she sat in the salon, waiting for her hair to be cut, slightly permed and curled, there were several men staring through the window. Letty, enjoying the attention, waved at them and smiled. She was now a woman on fire and drowning in a sea of self-indulgence as she felt that she had suddenly found the power to manipulate and control men and get anything she wanted from them.

Looking in the mirror at her immaculately trimmed hair and the slight curls that seemed to flutter a bit when she shook her head, Letty felt pleased and empowered. As she stood, she was enthralled by the way she looked. She realized that she was a beautiful woman and that the world was now at her feet. The new Letty would put that old Letty away and move forward toward a new tomorrow that would make her the envy of all women and make men beg for her attention. It was as if a horrid, grotesque, hideous caterpillar had sit down in that chair, and from it raised a magnificently beautiful butterfly.

J. Wayne Frye

LYNTON CURLS HER HAIR

As Letty was getting her hair cut, back in the Philippines, Wayne and Lynton were preparing for their last few days together. Now Lynton, at one time, was an extraordinary Contralto (Kontralto) singer and dancer who sometimes performed in Philippine shopping malls. Wayne had never heard her sing, but this day she was scheduled to appear at the SM Mall in Dasmarinas City where she was booked for an afternoon performance. As she prepared for the performance, Wayne sat in the dressing room admiring her fine form so much that Lynton turned to him and said, "How can I get dressed with you leering at me? You are a dirty old man."

Wayne, smiling, said, "Yes I am, and proud of it."

They laughed and Wayne noticed that as she ran her fingers through her hair, she had a look of disgust on her face. She really wanted some curl to her hair, but she was a typical Filipino with black, straight, long hair.

LYNTON CURLS HER HAIR

Wayne walked with her to the amphitheatre where she pranced like a gazelle onto the stage as he took a seat in the front row. She flashed that gorgeous smile and waved hello, the band began to play and she starting singing:

Back when I was a child,
Before life removed all the innocence,
My father would lift me high,
And dance with my mother and me and then spin me
around til I fell asleep.

Then up the stairs he would carry me
And I knew for sure I was loved.
If I could get another chance
Another walk, another dance with him
I'd play a song that would never ever end and how I
would love, love to dance,
to dance with my father again

When I and my mother would disagree,
To get my way I would run from her to him.
He'd make me laugh just to comfort me.

J. Wayne Frye

LYNTON CURLS HER HAIR

Yeah, yeah, then finally make me do just what my

mama said.

Later that night when I was asleep

He left a dollar under my sheet

Never dreamed that he would be gone from me.

If I could steal one final glance,

One final step, one final dance with him

I'd play a song that would never ever end,

'Cause I'd love, love, love, love to dance with my

father again.

Sometimes I'd listen outside her door

And I'd hear how my mama cried for him.

I pray for her even more than me.

I pray for her even more than me.

I know, I'm praying for much too much,

But could you send back the only man she loved?

I know you don't do it usually dear Lord she's dying

to dance with my father again.

Every night I fall asleep and this is all I ever dream.

J. Wayne Frye   99

LYNTON CURLS HER HAIR

I know You don't do it usually,
But dear Lord she's dying to dance with my father
again. Dance with my father again.

Wayne was a man who had been tempered by war when he served in the military at the end of the Vietnam War as an intelligence analyst. He felt the pain of men lying on the battlefield wounded and dying as they cried like babies for their mothers. Although sensitive, he was not one given to crying easily, but that night as he listened to Lynton sing, tears welt up in his eyes as he felt the sensitivity in her voice as each word seemed to pierce his heart, making him realize how acutely kind and caring this woman was. He looked at her hair that was bouncing about as she pranced from one side of the stage to the other. He smiled and thought about how much she wanted curly hair to make it flow gently and serenely while she cavorted about. He knew something that he must keep a secret until Valentine's Day, which was less than a month away.

LYNTON CURLS HER HAIR

After her performance, Wayne jokingly said, "If you had that curly hair, I bet you could have sung it better."

Lynton, used her favourite phrase, "Of course."

Laughing, the two of them strolled toward Wayne's favourite place to eat, Kentucky Fried Chicken. Standing at the counter, Wayne turned to her and said, "That song touched my heart, and I know now you are the most beautiful woman inside I have every known. Lynton, I love you so much."

There are moments in life when all the stars in the sky seem to be perfectly aligned, when everything in heaven and earth seems in perfect harmony. There are moments that mark your life. Moments when you realize nothing will ever be the same and time is divided into two parts: before this and after this. For Wayne and Lynton this was that moment. The diminutive Lynton at 5:2, was towered over by the 6:2 Wayne. She looked up at him affectionately, ignoring the clerk who placed their order on the counter, and she said with empathic determination something that she would say many times again, "I love you more!"

How does one describe love? It defies all explanation. As a gay activist once said to a minister who was pointing the finger of condemnation at him and his lover, "You can't chose whom you love. Jesus loved everyone, even his enemies." Wayne and Lynton loved each other. Some pointed at their age difference and made derisive comments, but when Wayne tried to get her to consider their age difference as a detriment to the romance, Lynton just said, "I would love you if you were 100 years old. I don't care what you look like. I don't care how virile you are. I don't care how much money you have. Whether I have you for a minute, an hour, a day, a year or a decade, I will love you until I take my last breath."

CHAPTER 6

HIS HEART AND SOUL WERE WITH HER

How I love the hair
On my lady so fair.
She has a mysterious beauty,
That I can never resist.
Her hair is like a golden mist
That shines and glistens,
In the sunset of my years.
A hair as smooth as silk,
That cascades over her shoulders

LYNTON CURLS HER HAIR

Gently resting, awaiting my touch.
She comforts my weary soul
Like a lullaby that brings sleep.
Her hair blooms and I fawn
Over it as I greet the gentle dawn.

There are a number of reasons why society often frowns on May-December romances. Those who degrade it see money as the motivating factor, sometimes referred to as the gold digger syndrome. This type of relationship is not the norm, so like anything that deviates from the norm in a conformist society, it is questioned, because too many people look through a prism distorted by prejudices in a world where everyone is expected to conform to a set of standards imposed by those who see themselves as the guardians of morality. For example, in the USA, ridiculousness often prevails over common sense. Do not deviate from the norm there or you can wind up in jail. Stand against the tyranny of conquest, question the merits of capitalism, defy convention and somehow you are a traitor to the American way. Those in power fear a public that is not acquiescent.

LYNTON CURLS HER HAIR

It took Wayne awhile to realize that love does not just come along. It is actually a rare commodity. Lynton was a woman who believed in fate and always said that she and Wayne were destined to be together, as that was the reason she and her boyfriend broke up, and the reason Wayne's wife ran away with another man. As Lynton was looking in a store window, coldness seemed to creep in all about them as if something evil was happening somewhere. They both looked at one another and Wayne, who had lived his young life in Asheboro, North Carolina, for some unknown reason had the town square of Asheboro flash across his mind, but there was something wrong with the picture, something that was sad and foreboding. The town square was engulfed in darkness and there was a dreary mist hanging over it. He shook his head a bit as if to clear the image from his mind. He said, "I know you think fate is why we are together and that is good, but don't you think fate can be bad, too?

"Fate is a hunter for good and evil," said Lynton, as she gently took Wayne's hand. Fate can find an evil person to perpetrate vile wickedness or it can find a good person to bring light to darkness. You are a good person who has brought me the light of your love."

The two lover's strolled through the mall, and Lynton stopped to look in a store window where a mannequin had long, wavy, slightly curly hair similar to what she wanted. Wayne could see the fascination in her gaze. She said nothing, but Wayne sensed the longing in her heart. Again, he filed it away for reference.

In Asheboro, Letty was thoroughly enjoying her new hairstyle and the attention she was now receiving from men. Her world changed so dramatically that she asked to stay awhile longer, and the request was granted. Now, to understand what happened later, we need to go back to the day Letty got her hair cut. You see, little incidents might seem quiet innocuous, but they can be precursors to what lies ahead for us whether it deals with fate or not. In Letty's case, something would occur that would alter her life and the lives of many who knew her.

LYNTON CURLS HER HAIR

She looked down at her hair that lay on the floor for just a second and she said to the stylist, "That is the old Letty on the floor. My shyness, my inept way of socializing is there in a heap." Then she looked in the mirror and saw a beautiful woman, a skilled, artful dancer in the waltz of seduction. As the stylist removed the smock from Letty, she arose as if a different person was getting out of the chair. She was leaving behind the old Letty and embracing a new, better Letty.

She paid her bill and noticed three boys she knew standing outside. She defiantly and boldly strolled out of the salon head held high with a look of egotistical assurance. Her stride bespoke of a woman with self-confidence and an air of sophistication. She was greeted by the three boys who praised her new look, but there was a thin bearded old man standing to their right just staring at her. He was a dirty, disgusting creature who reeked of odour so badly that it seemed to penetrate her nostrils from ten feet away.

LYNTON CURLS HER HAIR

She looked at him and with her now transformed personality, said, "You disgusting creature. What are you staring at?

He replied, "People see what they want to see." Then he stood there silently for a few seconds, and Letty noticed that his hair was dishevelled and on each side it had been clumped up and knotted by debris that had gathered there. The more she looked, the more she noticed that those clumps were almost forming a halo as the sun glistened on his head. The old man smiled through rotted teeth as he pointed a skinny finger directly at her. His words were carefully chosen and unexpectedly articulate. "Listen to me little missy, vanity is the hobgoblin of doom. You cut your hair today, but more than strands of hair fell to the floor. You also cut out the good heart you once had. There will be a reckoning coming, and you will wish that you had not let your kindness, generosity, sympathetic and kind-hearted nature be cut along with your hair. You will look back on this day with great woe."

J. Wayne Frye

LYNTON CURLS HER HAIR

The boys all laughed at the old man as Letty said, "Come on boys and escort me home. This old man is tiresome."

As they left, the old man, almost whispering, said, "Mark my words young woman, a day of reckoning is close at hand."

Again the four laughed and Letty signalled for them to turn around as she was now going to give the old man a real tongue-lashing. They all turned simultaneously, but the old man was not there. It was as if he had vanished into thin air.

While Letty was busy displaying her newfound vanity, in the Philippines, Wayne and Lynton were going to her friend Ingrid's home. As always, Lynton stopped to get something special for Ingrid and her mom, because those two had been so kind to her when she was down and out, and if you ever did Lynton a favour, it was never forgotten. Hers was a genuine appreciation with no caveats.

LYNTON CURLS HER HAIR

Whereas Letty was now just as vain as Mary, Lynton, on the other hand, despite her natural beauty, assured manner and success, always said, "I am just a simple girl with humble origins, humble means and humble wishes." Vanity was a word not in her vocabulary.

Each individual affects the course of mankind, like a rock you throw into the ocean affects the tide ever so slightly but a million rocks might cause a Tsunami. Words hurled and the actions manifested also have a cumulative effect. One humble individual can often altar people's lives through humility. Lynton was that solitary mind that refused to bow to recriminations. She had suffered many indignities in her life, but the perpetrators of those indignities were usually surprised when she simply ignored them rather than getting into the fray. She always said, "I do not waste my time and energy on those who have a closed mind, a hard heart and mush for brains. Arguing with people who have no vision let's your own vision slowly slip away."

LYNTON CURLS HER HAIR

On the day Wayne left the Philippines, Lynton's friends, Channa and Ingrid, came by to take them to the airport. Channa was a prim and proper statuesque beauty with ramrod posture and long, lithe legs that had captivated many men over the years. She saw Lynton as more like a sister than a friend, and the two of them had great admiration for one another. Channa's precise diction gave her an air of sophistication as she valued manners, comportment and appropriateness.

Ingrid, on the other hand, was less formal acting than Channa. She had a penchant for sublime humour with a somewhat devil-may-care attitude. She, too, was striking and stunning in looks with a statuesque frame and chiselled, soft lips that made most men wonder what it would be like to kiss them. She freely admitted she enjoyed the attention of men and saw no shame in it. She was truly a free spirit. If personality is an unbroken series of successful gestures, then there was something gorgeous about her, some heightened sensitivity to the nature of life and she possessed a gift for hope, and a romantic readiness to embrace those who were suitable pursuers.

As Channa drove Lynton and Wayne to the Manila Airport, with Wayne's arms around a despondent Lynton who could not bear the thought of him leaving her, he said, "What a lucky man I am to be out with three beautiful women tonight." Of course, for him, the most beautiful was Lynton, who had a natural beauty that seemed to flow from deep within. There was goodness about her beauty. Yes, she was sensual, but sensual in a naïve schoolgirl sort of way. She brought out the natural protective instincts in men, particularly in Wayne, whose advanced age made him long to protect her from harm. She was so sweet, so kind, so caring, so unassuming that her demeanour almost made you want to erect a barrier around her so that no one could ever break her heart or give her cause for worry. As she wiped moisture from her dark brown eyes, Wayne knew he had found his Shangri La in her warm arms and that there would never be another lover in his life, because all others would pale in comparison.

The journey seemed like they were taking a road to sorrow, as they both longed not to part. The bond between them was like a rose pedal drifting in a clear stream heading out to sea. They had never imagined that such profound bonding would occur in such a short time. Looking at the two, one could not help but wonder if even death would not keep them apart. It seemed that no barrier was too large for them to overcome, so confident were they in each other's love. All you had to do was observe the way they gazed upon one another to understand the depth of these two people's affection. Between them was a light that lit up the darkest corridors of loneliness and shone with a celestial glow that even God would, no doubt, envy. These two were the sizzle in the passion of life. They were the serenity of a tropical isle where trials and tribulations melted into harmonious contentment.

LYNTON CURLS HER HAIR

Of course, in a world where disharmony between countries and various interest groups is often the norm, Lynton was not allowed to enter the airport and escort Wayne to the gate due to the intense security measures that make travelers feel like they are all at the mercy of the miscreants who are fighting to free themselves from what they perceive as the suppression of their rights by the USA and the corporations that country serves. Standing at the entrance to the airport, Lynton melted in Wayne's arms and felt the warmth of his love seem to emanate from deep within. This man adored her. She felt so safe in his arms and knew that she would feel so alone without him by her side. He accepted her without reservations. His was a love that knew no bounds. His was a love beyond judgement. He saw no wrong in her, only good. As she fought back tears, because she didn't want to make it difficult on him, her breathing became laboured. Wayne bent down and whispered in her ear, "Lynton it will be O.K. Things are going to work out. Be patient and we will be together. I promise."

J. Wayne Frye

LYNTON CURLS HER HAIR

Wayne slipped a piece of paper in her hand and said in a soft, almost whispering voice, "It is my farewell poem my darling. Read it often after I am gone and remember how much you are loved by me. Each minute, each hour, each day is like an eternity without you."

I can see your cherub face when I close my eyes.
The whistling wind brings me your voice.
Memories of you float within me
Like vintage grapes on the vine.
Nothing is harder than leaving you behind.
Each step away tugs the strings of my heart.
Illusions are fostered deep within.
Reflections of your face shadow my sanity.
Every single step away from you takes an eternity.
Games of illusions are played by my mind.
My tears fall like rain, washing reality away,
Blowing whispers of the love we share
Blending the present, yesterday and tomorrow.
We danced among the stars singing a heavenly tune
As in your essence I float in celestial charm.

LYNTON CURLS HER HAIR

Tasting your lips and your love made me whole
With a yearning embrace that caresses my soul.
I recall our time together with no sorrow,
As within my heart I have hope for tomorrow.

Wayne kissed her once more and said goodbye. He was leaving, but only his body was going, because his heart and soul were still with her.

CHAPTER 7
THE VAIN BURN IN HELL

Letty excitedly enjoyed her new found popularity, but she could not get that scraggily old man out of her mind. Why was he there at that particular time to destroy her newfound glorious embrace of that which she had longed for? Who was he? What was he? Was he an oracle, a prognosticator of doom?

Hey, she was the new Letty, and nothing would get in the way of her newfound confidence. She was going to enjoy the last few weeks of summer and bask in the gloriousness that awaited her. She looked in the mirror at her hair and it seemed to glow with great radiance, as it was now the centrepiece on the great table of opportunity that was laid before her filled with an array of delectable delights to gratify her ever-expanding egomania. The aim of an ego is not to see something wisely, but to be something exalted. That is its folly.

Ego is not necessarily a bad thing, as we all need to feel good about ourselves, but when ego supplants common courtesy and when an individual begins to aggrandize and exalt themselves in their own minds, perspective is sacrificed at the altar of self-indulgence. Letty was confusing confidence with egotistical arrogance. A simple hairstyle change was also changing her from a kind, caring person into an unrecognizable ogre with a hardened heart filled with the arrogance of self-importance. What she saw in the mirror was a beautiful young woman, but the truth was she had become ugly.

LYNTON CURLS HER HAIR

Suddenly, as she stared in the mirror admiring her hair, the room seemed to darken, an undulating light appeared in the mirror and gradually a blurry image began to crystallize. Oh no, she thought, as a ring of fire was framing the face of that old man outside the salon. His eyes were beet red and his nostrils were breathing fire. Then a bony finger arose in front of his face pointing directly at her. The words seemed to sear into her brain: "Woman, virtue would go far if vanity did not keep it company. You have sacrificed virtue for self-indulgent vanity and the price is too high to pay."

Letty wanted to scream but the sound would not come out of her mouth. She just stood there staring in the mirror as the image slowly faded away. The room was silent except for the sound of her own heavy breathing. She said to herself, "I am hallucinating. Sure, all the excitement caused by my new hairstyle and newfound confidence has just been too much for me." She looked in the mirror admiringly at her beautiful hair, smiling confidently as her eyes twinkled with excitement, because there was a country club dance that Friday night. It would be her first dance since the style change and she would be the bell of the ball. Yeah, the bell of the ball.

The prophets of doom should be taken seriously, but a vision in the mirror was nonsense thought Letty, as she prepared for what she assumed would be the crowning glory of her new self. She was about to overwhelm all the young men with her beauty and sophistication. She was a girl who had finally arrived, and look out world, because she was about to strut her stuff.

The equally vain Mary knocked on Letty's door and said, "Come on girl. We have men waiting to be vamped."

Transformations are not always pleasing to the eye, but Letty opened the door and Mary was astonished. All she could say was, "Letty."

LYNTON CURLS HER HAIR

Now, so vain was Letty that she just smiled and said, "Yes, I know I am gorgeous, and it is all because I decided to get my hair styled. My dear Mary, your nastiness motivated me and I thank you. However, it has made you the second most beautiful woman who will be at the ball tonight. You may leave without me, because I plan to make a grand entrance."

Mary, aghast at the arrogance of Letty, just stood there with her mouth hanging open. She realized that her nastiness had created a monster. It was one of the few times that she was at a loss for words. Mary turned and forlornly headed downstairs. She was now reaping what she had sown.

Letty felt good inside, because she had put Mary in her place. Now, it was Letty who was at the top of the food chain, and she was thoroughly enjoying herself. The mirror prognosticator of doom was not going to interfere with her good time. Anyway, it was an illusion, a hallucination, she told herself.

LYNTON CURLS HER HAIR

As Letty was preparing to flaunt her stuff on the dance floor, Wayne reflected on Lynton and how much faith she had put in him. For days after Wayne left, Lynton mourned almost uncontrollably, because she missed Wayne so much, and across the ocean, Wayne was also morose. Then, there was one time when Lynton questioned Wayne's fidelity. Distance can create suspicious minds and after a few weeks away from each other, they both seemed concerned about fidelity. When Lynton stopped calling Wayne three times a day due to some problems at work, he thought that perhaps she had found herself a more suitable and younger man. His doubts were unfounded, but he was so attached, so dependent on Lynton that he had a difficult time coping with the separation. These difficulties did not drive a wedge between them, but it did make them both leery. One day in particular, Lynton seemed overly sensitive when Wayne helped his ex-wife with some problems she was having. It is never easy being apart from a loved one, and this day was one where jealousy did rear its ugly head, but by the end of their morning conversation, all was well. Yet, in Wayne's heart was a longing to make Lynton understand just how devoted he was to her. The thought of harming her, doing her any injustice was simply unfathomable in his mind, and he wanted to make her understand that. For that reason, he wrote her a poem after their conversation.

I SHED NOT A TEAR

The woman I loved the most in my youth lay dying.
I thought our love could even cheat death,
but it was not to be.
By her bedside, I saw my grandmother
Gasp desperately for a breath
That never came, but I shed not a tear.

I was tempered by a war in a foreign land.
My 19 year old friend lay dying on wet ground.
I pleaded with him to hang on.
The end came, and I shed not a tear.

I suffered a gaping wound in my hip
From the blade of a foe's bayonet.
Blood streamed out like a raging river.
In excruciating pain, I shed not a tear.

I have battled furiously on the hockey rink.
Tooth half out, jaw shattered, fingers broken,
Concussions endured for the sake of the game.
All those agonies and I shed not a tear.

LYNTON CURLS HER HAIR

I watched my dear mother battle
cancer for seven long years.
The pain at times was unbearable.
She finally heeded the call of eternity.
I preached her funeral and shed not a tear.

My father lay in the hospital dying of emphysema
Almost pleading for the relief of death.
It mercifully came one dark day.
Through it all, I shed not a tear.

Today, a diminutive 5:2 woman
questioned my fidelity.
I had not betrayed her, but she was unsure.
The thought of hurting her was more
than I could bear.
I shed a tear! I shed a tear!

From that day forward, neither one of them ever questioned each other's fidelity. They begin to comprehend that their love was predicated on such a solid foundation of mutual respect and trust that it was unshakable.

It was nearing February 14, and Wayne had filed an idea away in the back of his mind that he hoped would prove not only a great surprise, but truly touch Lynton's heart.

J. Wayne Frye

LYNTON CURLS HER HAIR

Wayne called a hair salon that Lynton had said was the best in the metro Manila area and did a great job with the laser curling of hair. He knew Lynton's day off work was Wednesday, so he made an appointment at 9:00 AM, which happened to be Valentine's Day. An e-mail to Ingrid asked her to read Lynton a poem he wrote to her at 7:00 AM on Valentine's Day and to have Channa pick her up and take her to the hair appointment. All was set for a surprise that would touch Lynton deeply, and make her realize just how much Wayne loved her.

Now, it seems that Valentine's was not only a day when Wayne would surprise Lynton, but it would also be a day when Letty would face the consequences of letting vanity rule her heart and mind. As she walked into the ballroom, all eyes were on the new Letty, who had a regal bearing that made people look up and take notice. Warren Adams, without taking his eyes off Letty, said to Mary, who was standing beside him, "Absolutely amazing. Incredible. What a beautiful woman."

LYNTON CURLS HER HAIR

Hour after hour Letty was bombarded with requests to dance as all the men fawned over her, and her hair seemed to shimmer with life, almost as if it was a separate entity. Men sneaked touches of it and felt its soft, lustrous, velvety texture. She was basking in the glory she thought she had achieved with her hair. She would repeatedly go to the washroom and stare at her hair, flip her head back and forth to watch it cascade down to her shoulders. The curls seemed to be alive, to be shouting her magnificence as a woman. Her vanity was overpowering her. She became mesmerized as she stared at the image in the mirror. How beautiful she was. Oh, she had the world at her feet, and it was all because of her curly hair.

Three hours later, while Warren was standing passively watching the dancers and wondering why Mary had seemingly disappeared, an unrelated perception began to creep slowly upon him as he watched the vibrant Letty whirl about the dance floor. He closed his eyes, opened them and looked

J. Wayne Frye

again. She danced every dance with a different man. Men were all standing in line wanting to be next. Strangely, you could see all the men, as they danced with her, somehow manage to clandestinely feel her hair. The hair was like a magnet. Even Letty herself could not keep from running her hands through it periodically. As she did so, she got a radiant glow about her, almost as if the hair was omniscient.

Warren was distinctly surprised when Letty danced near him and gave him a provocative wink over the right shoulder of her current dance partner. Warren regarded her intently. Yes, she was pretty, no beautiful; and that night she seemed especially vivacious and extremely confident. He couldn't take his eyes off her hair. There was something magical about it. And her dark black dress blended in perfectly with her coal black hair. He remembered that he had thought her mildly pretty when she first came to town, before he had realized that she was boring, but now that didn't seem to matter. Yes, she was not the same Letty.

His thoughts zigzagged back to Mary. Where was she? Then, he caught a glimpse of her on the veranda out of his right eye. She was leaning over and whispering something to Jim Johnson. There was something up. Mary was planning something – no doubt about it. Why was she ignoring him? She meandered over and Warren said, "Where have you been? What were you whispering to Jimmy about?"

Very empathetically, Mary said, "None of your business. However, I'll just say that Miss Uppity," and she pointed at Letty, "out there on the dance floor is about to get her comeuppance. It won't be long now."

Warren sighed. Mary's vindictiveness was legendary. Cross her and you paid. He looked straight into her eyes, but she wasn't looking at him. She was honed in like a beacon on Letty, as she was dancing with yet another boy. Half unconsciously he took a step back from her, and hesitated. Then he said to himself that she was capable of vile evil.

LYNTON CURLS HER HAIR

As he backed away from Mary, almost mesmerized, by her glaring stare in Letty's direction, he bumped into Bill Steadman. "Pardon me," said Warren.

"No problem" said Bill as he gazed in Letty's direction. "Check out that Letty. Wow man, we overlooked a real winner with that girl. I want some of that action. What a girl. I don't know how I ignored such a beautiful woman all this time."

Mary very slowly moved toward the master ballroom light switch, still staring at Letty with eyes that were like sharp daggers. It was 12 midnight – the witching hour thought Mary, and I am going to get me a witch. With one hand on the electric-light switch in the hall, she turned to take a last look at Letty's sparkling, shiny, radiant hair. Thus began the evil that would be talked about in Asheboro for many years, an evil perpetrated by simply getting a haircut and a curl, but in reality, it was much more than that, it was a curl of insidious evil.

LYNTON CURLS HER HAIR

Vanity in and of itself is a manifestation of self-indulgence with an almost obsessive excess of pride in one's appearance, qualities, abilities and achievements. Letty had simply refined the art of vanity in a brief time to a level never even imagined by the terribly vain Mary. Letty was like a high priestess standing on an altar making a human sacrifice to her own glory. She was prepared to make each man grovel for one touch of her soft, silky smooth hair.

All girls dream of being popular. It is perfectly natural, but all girls do not dream equally. Since Letty's visit to the hair salon she had dreamed in the darkest corners of the night. The dusty recesses of her mind harboured a newfound vanity that was beyond the norm. It was obsessive. She awakened each day with a surge in her vanity to the point of being on dangerously unholy ground. She had developed contempt for those she now deemed beneath her. She was headed for disaster, because vanity goes before a great fall.

J. Wayne Frye

LYNTON CURLS HER HAIR

Mary had her hand on the main ballroom light switch. One flick and the room would be in darkness. One flick and the curtain of revenge would fall on Letty, and she would know that crossing Mary was a path to doom.

Meanwhile, in Wayne's room, where he did his writing, he lay on the sofa thinking of his dear Lynton and how surprised she would be with her Valentine's present. No flowers, no candy, just an unusual gift from the heart. And it would also prove to her just how much she meant to a man who still had problems fathoming how such a sweet, kind-hearted, compassionate, beautiful young woman could love an old man so much. It was almost incomprehensible to him. It was far beyond his realm of understanding. He longed for her. He pined for her. He ached for her. His thoughts seemed to float in the air, and soar upward as if breaking free and sailing a calm sea into the serenity of love so deep, so abiding, so fathomless that the angels in heaven envied their affection for one another.

LYNTON CURLS HER HAIR

Words sometimes came hard to Wayne, but not this night. Words formed a pattern in his mind and they flowed like fine wine from a bottle uncorked with passion and poured into an exquisite crystal glass that sparkled and glistened with rapturous tenderness. This was a night of adulation, fervour and devotion. He whispered the words aloud, as if Lynton were beside him and if they were spoken too loud they might lose their tenderness. They flowed not from his mind, but from his heart, a heart that beat with the rhythm of affection for his dear Lynton, and each word hung in the air, floating softly like a vapour in a dewy mist of love.

As I lie on my bed staring at the ceiling
my head is spinning with thoughts of you.
I hear your voice throughout the day
telling me that you love me.

Your voice is a whisper in the wind,
desperately crying your affection to lend.
I long for you to hold me near,
but when I look around you're not here.

J. Wayne Frye

LYNTON CURLS HER HAIR

At night I pine for your smile,
and I whimper alone in disharmony,
longing for just one mere sight
of you who brings me delight.

I miss hearing you proclaim your love.
I miss your captivating smile.
You are a symphony within my heart.
Emptiness prevails. Oh, how I hate being apart.

What was about to happen in Asheboro would be an example of how vanity can destroy a person's soul. Letty was a victim of vanity, but so was Mary, who unbeknownst to her was fulfilling the prophecy of the old man who pointed the boney finger of doom at Letty, trying to warn her about the folly of vanity. There was cataclysmic calamity brewing courtesy of Mary and Jim Johnson.

Mary moved her hand to the master light switch with anticipatory delight. She glanced over at the open doorway to the veranda and there was a scraggily-glad old thin man standing at the entrance. His hair was dirty and there were those customary two clumps on each side, almost forming that aforementioned halo around his head. He looked horrible and there was a putrid smell of death that seemed to suddenly penetrate Mary's nostrils. She remembered once seeing a painting entitled "Angel of Death." She recognized the man from the painting, but it couldn't be. The painting was done by one of the Dutch masters in 1650. As the old man raised his boney right finger and pointed at Mary, he closed the doors with his left hand.

Mary felt sick as she watched the scraggily glad old man gently close the doors as if performing a task of great concern, take a rope and wrap it around the two outer doorknobs so the doors could not be opened. She wanted to shout, to scream that terror was about to be unleashed, but she stood like a stone wall unable to move. A voice began to hum in her head, conveying not with words, but with just sound, a coming doom. It was only for a brief period, for it stopped almost as quickly as it started. Then, she observed the old man; his beet red eyes glowing like the fires of hell, peering through the glass door looking directly at her and his lips were moving, forming one word that he was repeating over and over. A deadly nausea crept upon her. What was he saying thought Mary? What was he saying? Oh my God! The word he was mouthing sent cold chills down her spine. Yes, he was mouthing the word "death" over and over again.

Suddenly Mary's stoic countenance was arrested and she sprang from her trance. Hallucinations she thought. It was nothing but worry that she was about to go too far in combating the vanity of Letty. There was no old man. There were no ropes around door knobs. There was just going to be the fun of giving Letty her comeuppance. Mary flicked the lights out, and then back on just as Letty started up the main staircase grasping the banister. For the first time in Letty's life she was exhausted from dancing.

LYNTON CURLS HER HAIR

She felt her way holding the banister, and there was a glimmer of moonlight dancing about through a small window at the top of the landing. Suddenly Letty's hair began to give-off a red glow and at the top of the stairs, waiting for her was none other than the shy and soft-spoken Chuck Pauly who was framed in the dancing moonlight. In almost a whisper he said, "Letty, you were much prettier before you got that infernal curl in your hair, because then you were real. Now you are a fake. There is no beauty whatsoever in a vain person who is self-indulgent. Frankly, now you are ugly."

Right behind Chuck was Jim Johnson and Mary shouted the cue for him to act on their plot. Throughout the room the words shouted by Mary seemed to vibrate all about, echoing a truism of catastrophic condemnation that was, in fact, true of most of the people there that night, but particularly true of Letty and Mary, who were prime examples of how vanity can bring those who exalt themselves above all others ultimately to their knees.

J. Wayne Frye

LYNTON CURLS HER HAIR

The words spoken by Mary were profound, and they were symbolic of that which is true when ego trumps humility. "Vanity is the devil's trap."

With that cue, Jim Johnson stepped around Chuck and Letty caught just a glimpse of what was in his right hand. Fear overwhelmed her and a scream started its way up her throat but got caught half way and just hung their idly waiting for a release that never came. What Jim had in his hand was not meant to cause a calamitous event. It was intended as a way to bring embarrassment to Letty, and let her recognize the folly of her vanity. Of course, it was perpetrated by Mary, whose vanity nearly surpassed that of Letty. She and Jim had been partners in chemistry lab, and they had studied how a mixture of sodium valborate with sugar and sulphuric acid would make hair go limp and lifeless. The only problem was they confused sodium chlorate with sodium valborate. Add sodium chlorate with sugar and sulphuric acid and when exposed to air, the result is fire.

LYNTON CURLS HER HAIR

Jim removed the cap from the bottle and tossed it on Letty's hair. Finally, Letty's scream came out as her gorgeous hair lit up like a comet streaking through the midnight sky. What was intended as a prank to make Letty's hair less appealing turned into a catastrophe.

Jim, standing there in shock, could not move. Suddenly the flames engulfed him and he ran down the stairs screaming, the flames leaped from him to engulf several people who were ascending and descending the stairs. He collapsed at the bottom of the stairs in ashes, but the flames were now leaping from him and devouring all those who were standing on the dance floor in shock. Pandemonium broke out as Mary stood transfixed on Letty whose hair was ablaze, but it was not burning her. It was as if Letty were made of stone and was impervious to the fire. Suddenly, bolts of fire leaped out from her hair as she turned toward the ballroom. The bolts zapped about engulfing person after person in flames. Letty, no longer screaming, turned and

J. Wayne Frye

stared down at Mary. Her eyes were now aglow with fiery redness. Mary turned to run toward the door, but a bolt of fire zapped from Letty's hair blocking her way forward. She turned to the right and another bolt blocked her. Then she turned to the left and a bolt struck her in the back, sitting her ablaze. As Mary screamed, an evil grin crept across Letty's face. She raised her head toward the window where the moonlight was now dancing more intensely, almost as if delighted over the carnage that was laying low all those who pranced about in their finery thinking that they were exalted above others. Through it all, one person was spared. Still standing at the top of the stairs, so shocked he could not move was the shy, reticently sheepish, non-vain Chuck Pauly. His mouth hung open and he began to tremble when Letty slowly turned toward him with her red piercing eyes still aglow and her hair now only simmering with fire. The crackling sound of her hair burning sent shivers through him as he prepared to die. He breathed heavily, but he was no longer fearful. He was dead and he knew it.

LYNTON CURLS HER HAIR

As bodies piled up at the locked door, a powerful almost God-like voice came out of Letty's mouth and said, "It is dangerous for mean, pity minds to venture themselves within the sphere of greatness. The vain are blinded by the splendour of wealth and the arrogance of status. The vain sell their virtue. They smell of the corruption of what is good. There is no greater evil than vanity. I am proof of that, and I am paying the price"

Letty collapsed onto the landing in front of Chuck, her ashes simmering with the corruption of vanity. Chuck bowed his head and descended slowly down the stairs and walked past the dead smouldering bodies. He reached the doors and the rope locking the outer doorknobs, as if by magic, fell off. He went out the veranda door into the dark night that wrapped itself around him like a warm blanket. The moonlight shone down upon him, framing him in its light, as if to say "The virtuous shall be wrapped in the light of heaven, while the vain burn in hell."

J. Wayne Frye

LYNTON CURLS HER HAIR

EPILOGUE
PARADISE IN EACH OTHERS ARMS

The carnage in Asheboro was an example of vanity gone wild, but in Cavite, Philippines, Lynton, who spent each day in complete humility as she treated all with kindness and never let vanity rear its ugly head, was awakened at 7:30 A.M. by a phone call from her friend Ingrid. She was about to receive a message that would forever endear Wayne to her as she would realize that she had the love of a man who adored her beyond her wildest dreams. He had instructed Ingrid to read a short poem to her.

LYNTON CURLS HER HAIR

Ingrid, who longed for a man to love her as Wayne loved Lynton, read Wayne's words to Lynton with great feeling and emotion.

"Lynton, Wayne asked me to call you and read this."

THERE IS AN OCEAN BETWEEN US
BUT THAT CANNOT KEEP US APART
PLEASE KNOW ON THIS SPECIAL DAY
YOU HAVE MY HEART

My dear Lynton, I know you want your hair curled. I have made an appointment for you at a salon to have it done. Channa will pick you up at 8:30. This is my Valentine's Day gift to you. You are a humble and kind person who deserves a special treat once in awhile. I love you!

Through tears of joy, Lynton said to Ingrid, "He loves me so much. I cannot believe he did this. I told him long ago how I desired to have my hair laser curled, and he waited to give me this on a special day. I will treasure this day until I take my last breath. I love him so much."

Ingrid, who herself shed a few tears, replied, "I envy the love you two have for each other."

The nature of any couple's relationship depends upon a number of different factors including their personal histories and personalities, their views on relationships and the way that they interact and communicate with one another. For that reason, it is impossible to say definitively if a May-December romance is a "good thing" or a "bad thing." However, in Wayne and Lynton's case, that Valentine's day they were both like teenagers in love. The age difference was just a number, and it was a number that was meaningless to them in the grand scheme of things.

Lynton called Wayne as soon as Ingrid hung up, and through tears she said, "Baby, I love you so much," and then with a bit of levity, she continued, "and I know you love my beautiful body, but I also know you love the beauty inside me. I am not really a beautiful woman, and I know it. You keep telling me how beautiful I am, but you see me differently than anyone else. I am so thankful for what you have done. It is the best present anyone has ever given me. However, you never have to give me any material things, because you already have given me the greatest gift of all – your love."

After two and one half hours at the salon, Lynton went back to work with a special spring in her step and she felt euphoric with her new curls, but it wasn't the curls that put the spring in her step. It was the love of a man who made her a special gift of them. There are moments in everyone's life that stand out as a defining point, a definitive time when things are divided into a before and after. This was one of those times. Lynton's love for Wayne was not predicated on a gift, but on the love that made him want to do something special for her.

A radiant Lynton called Wayne on Skype and let him see her new hairdo. Unlike Letty, there would be no vanity on Lynton's part, just happiness that she had a man who loved her so much. They both cried. They were floating on a cloud of love in the heavenly bliss of happiness secure in the knowledge that together they had found paradise in each others arms.

The End

If You Liked This Book

Don't Miss These Young Readers Series Books

By

J. Wayne Frye

HOCKEY MANIA AND THE MYSTERY OF NANCY RUNNING ELK

And

HOW HOCKEY SAVED A JEW FROM THE HOLOCAUST: THE RUDI BALL STORY

LYNTON CURLS HER HAIR

The author with the real Lynton Globa Viñas at
the Club Gilligan's Island in Dasmarinas City,
Philippines, and taking this picture was the real Ingrid
Bautista with the real Channa Mendis beside her.

Don't miss the J. Wayne Frye book that explores
the extraordinary bravery of some notable
Native Americans who fought for justice against
the U.S. government.

POINTS OF REBELLION:
NORTH AMERICAN ABORIGINALS
WHO FOUGHT FOR JUSTICE

LYNTON CURLS HER HAIR

VOCABULARY

(Definitions from *Canadian Oxford Dictionary*)

PROLOGUE

disdain: a feeling of strong dislike or disapproval of someone or something you think does not deserve respect

CHAPTER 1

sedate: slow and relaxed/quiet and peaceful

minions: someone who is not powerful or important and who obeys the orders of a powerful leader or boss

probity: adherence to the highest principles and ideals

bastion: a place or system in which something (such as an old-fashioned idea) continues to survive (a stronghold)

harmoniousness: not experiencing disagreement or fighting

immutable: not capable of or susceptible to change

staid: serious, boring, or old-fashioned

adroitly: having or showing skill, cleverness, or resourcefulness in handling situations ostentatious: displaying wealth, knowledge, etc., in a way that is meant to attract attention, admiration, or envy

postulates: demand, claim/ to assume as a postulate or axiom

plaintive: expressing suffering or sadness : having a sad sound

CHAPTER 2

chagrin: a feeling of being frustrated or annoyed because of failure or disappointment

fastidious: very careful about how to do something

homage: respect or honour for something or somebody

epitome: a perfect example/ an example that represents or expresses something very well

grandeur: great and impressive quality

conventionality: a conventional usage, practice or thing

irrefutably: not able to be proved wrong/not cpable of neing refuted.

haughty: having or showing an insulting attitude by thinking they are better, smarter or more important

LYNTON CURLS HER HAIR

CHAPTER 3

deviltry: wickedness

cursory: rapidly and often superficially performed or produced or performed

façade: a way of behaving or appearing that gives other people a false idea of your true feelings or situation

dissipated: spread out, disappear, go away

promiscuous: including or involving too many people or things : not limited in a careful or proper way

disparage: to describe (someone or something) as

unimportant: weak, bad, etc.

CHAPTER 4

stolid: having or expressing little or no sensibility

livid: very angry

disdain: a feeling of strong dislike or disapproval of someone or something that does not deserve respect

acquiescent: tending to accept or allow what others want or demand

pariah: a person who is hated and rejected by other people

diligently: characterized by steady effort

pensive: musingly or dreamily thoughtful

abominably: causing disgust or hatred/ disagreeable or unpleasant

tedious: tiresome because of length or dullness

sequestered: apart from other people

laboriously: involving or characterized by hard or a very toilsome effort

chastised: inflict punishment or censure

urbane: polite and confident / somewhat formal or a bit fashionable

trepidation: a feeling of fear that causes you to hesitate because you think something bad or unpleasant is going to happen

ferret: an active and persistent search

simpatico: being on the same wavelength and congenial, sympathetic, agreeable

cognizant: aware of / knowledgeable of something especially through personal experience

scenario: a description of what could possibly happen

frivolities: a lack of seriousness / the quality or state of being silly trysts: an agreement (as between lovers) to meet

caveats: an explanation to prevent misinterpretation/ an explanation or warning that should be reflected on when you are doing or thinking about something

fathom: understand (a difficult problem or an enigmatic person) after much thought

statuesque: tall and beautiful

exude: to show (a quality, emotion, etc.) very clearly or strongly

ninnies: fool, simpleton

innocuous: not likely to bother or offend anyone

CHAPTER 5

traverse: route or way across or over

unscathed: wholly unharmed, not injured

ecstatic: of, relating to, or marked by ecstasy / very happy

pièce de résistance: the best or most important thing or event

abombinable: very bad or unpleasant

abeyance: suspension or inactivity

ascribe: to refer to a supposed cause, source, person

superficiality: only the obvious/no substance/depth

penchant: a strong and continued inclination

vamp: a seductive woman who exploits men with her charm

raucous: boisterously disorderly

contralto (kontralto): a singing voice having a range between tenor and mezzo-soprano

acquiescent: tending to accept or allow what other people want or demand

CHAPTER 6

mannequin: a figure shaped like a human body that is used for making or displaying clothes

innocuous: not likely to bother or offend anyone

precursors: something that comes before something else and that often leads to or influences its development

dishevelled: not neat or tidy

hobgoblin: something that causes fear or worry

simultaneously: existing or occurring at the same time

penchant: a strong liking for something or a strong tendency to behave in a certain way

sublime: not showy/beneath the surface

comportment: to behave in a manner conformable to what is right, proper, or expected

Shangri-La: a remote beautiful imaginary place where life approaches perfection

miscreants: depraved, villainous

oracle: a person through whom God speaks/an person who is venerated and respected for advice

CHAPTER 7

prognosticator: a person who foretells from signs or symptoms

egomania: quality or state of thinking very highly of yourself and flaunting it

aggrandize: to enhance the power, wealth, position, or reputation of

exalt: to praise highly

ogre: someone or something that is very frightening, cruel, or difficult to deal with

unfathomable: impossible to understand

predicated: affirm, assert or imply

clandestinely: secretly done or concealed

vivacious: lively and full of happiness

omniscient: Godlike, perceiving all things

emphatically: forceful, strongly expressive

comeuppance: deserved reward or just deserts, usually unpleasant

rapturous: full of, feeling, or manifesting ecstatic joy or delight

adulation: excessive devotion to someone; servile flattery

unbeknownst: unknown; unperceived

vindictiveness: strong desire to get back at someone

havoc: great destruction or devastation; ruinous damage

inadvertently: without knowledge or intent

putrid: having the odour of decaying flesh

Epilogue

carnage: the slaughter of a great number of people, butchery; massacre